Report On the Civil Establishments of Malta

CONTENTS.

	PAGE
Preliminary Observations (Pars. 1-4)	5
The Chief Secretary's Office (Pars. 22-31)	6
The Treasury (Pars. 32-37)	7
The Land Revenue and Public Works Department (Pars. 38-94)	8
The Customs Department (Pars. 95-109)	16
The Port Department (Pars. 110-127)	19
Police and Prisons (Pars. 128-150)	21
The Charitable Institutions (Pars. 151-184)	24
The Monte di Pietà and Savings Bank (Pars. 185-190)	31
The Public Libraries (Pars. 191-193)	32
The Government Printing Office (Pars. 194-200)	32
The Post Office (Pars. 201 and 202)	34
The Public Registry (Pars. 203-214)	35
The Inferior Courts (Pars. 215-237)	37
The Superior Courts (Pars. 238-272)	42
The Audit Office (Pars. 273-284)	48
Establishments (Pars. 285-306)	50
The English Language in Malta (Pars. 307-317)	56
Refund of Customs Duties (Pars. 318-322)	60
Summary of Suggestions (Pars. 323-340)	60

Plan of Malta and Gozo	Facing 8

APPENDICES.

A. Letter of Instructions	63
B. Government Property in Lands and Houses	64
C. Observations on the Judicial and Magisterial Establishments of Malta. (By Sir Antonio Micallef, K.C.M.G., LL.D.)	68
D. Proposed Changes in the Establishments.	75

REPORT

ON

THE CIVIL ESTABLISHMENTS OF MALTA.

OFFICE OF THE CROWN AGENTS FOR THE COLONIES,
DOWNING STREET, LONDON, 25th March, 1879.

SIR,
    I have the honour to report that, in compliance with your direction that I should make certain inquiries concerning the organisation and working of the Civil Establishments of Malta, as well as other subjects pointed out in Mr. Herbert's letter of the 12th of October last,* I at once proceeded to the Island, and spent more than three months in making the necessary investigations.

    * See Appendix A.

    2. Before setting forth in detail the conclusions at which I have arrived, and my grounds for the same, I may say generally, with reference to the principal object of my mission, that there appears to me room for only a limited reduction in the number of Government employés, consequent on alterations of system which I shall propose, and none in the salaries of the subordinate classes. After personal examination of nearly every member of the Civil Service, including its professional branches, I find that, as a rule, their duties are performed with care and attention, and that the remuneration given to them is so low as to render any abatement of it inexpedient. Indeed, if the recommendations I shall make as to economy in organisation and the rearrangement of some of the Departments are adopted, I consider that all, or nearly all, the saving thus effected in the number of employés may be judiciously applied in augmenting the stipends of those who remain. I shall recur to this subject after treating of the several Departments.

    3. Such observations as I have to offer on the other matters referred to in Mr. Herbert's letter will be most conveniently placed in later portions of this Report.

    4. I would here, however, premise that, though in the course of my remarks I shall have to touch upon various professional questions, both legal and medical, my references to these subjects will be as brief as I can make them with due regard to the task assigned to me. I feel that I should be exceeding my functions were I to recommend any important legislative changes, or any alteration in the principles upon which the affairs of the Island are managed; and I can only speak deferentially concerning either the propriety of furnishing so small a dependency with such elaborate arrangements as exist for the administration of justice and the distribution of medical and other charities, or the professional competence of the large number of officials who are entrusted with those duties. Yet it appears to me that the increased prosperity of the Colony will depend quite as much upon improvements in those respects as upon any changes that can be made in the condition of the Civil Service proper.

THE CHIEF SECRETARY'S OFFICE.

22. The importance of the position of the Chief Secretary to Government in Malta is increased by the fact that Her Majesty's representative is Commander of the Forces, as well as Governor in civil affairs. A large share of the Governor's attention being necessarily absorbed in military concerns, it is essential to the proper administration of the general business of the Island that he should have at his right hand an accurate informant, and a thoroughly competent adviser, on all matters of detail. In no colony is it to be expected that a Governor, whose residence is limited to a comparatively short period, can make adequate use of such capacities for government as he possesses without assistance from some one having longer experience, and more intimate acquaintance with the temperament and condition of the inhabitants and the exigencies and working of the public Departments, than are within his own range. This is especially the case in such a dependency as Malta, where the great majority of the population know nothing or next to nothing of the English language. The Chief Secretary is called upon not only to furnish the Governor with a correct view of the actual circumstances of the Island, but also to interpret to him all the wishes and complaints of more or less truly representative sections of the community, and to be his responsible agent, without usurping his power, in administering all civil affairs. I have recommended that the responsibilities in these respects now devolving upon him be lightened by the formation of an Executive Council. Of that Council, however, he will necessarily and properly be a prominent member, and it will naturally be his duty to see that all matters of importance are submitted to and duly discussed by it. He will also be at once relieved and assisted as regards some of the multifarious burdens now attached to his office if the proposals I shall hereafter make as to the appointment of a Finance Committee and a Contract Committee * be adopted. It is necessary that he should be possessed of great tact, patience and firmness, in order to deal successfully with the people of Malta, while his experience and ability should be such as to command their respect; and it is very desirable that he should be well acquainted with the Italian language. I do not think that the services of such an officer are likely to be obtained for less than a maximum salary of £1000 a year, and I recommend that the successor of the present Chief Secretary should receive a stipend not exceeding that amount.

23. In the Chief Secretary's Office there are now employed an Assistant, a Chief Clerk, and three other Clerks, whose aggregate salaries amount to £960 a year. This number is not excessive for the work at present done in the Department; but by relieving it of some details which interfere with its higher functions and which can as well be performed in subordinate offices, and by eliminating certain superfluities, a small saving may be effected with advantage.

24. The preparation of the Annual Blue Book, including the correction of proof-sheets, now nominally performed by the Chief Secretary, but which is really nothing more than a compilation made by Clerk No. 1 from Returns furnished by other Departments, as well as the management or editorship of the *Government Gazette*, might with propriety be placed in other hands.†

25. The Annual and Supplementary Estimates, at present drawn up by the Chief Clerk from statements prepared in the several Departments concerned, should also be dealt with elsewhere.‡

26. Letters from all public bodies, including the Judicial Establishments and representatives of the Church, should not be accepted if written in any other language than English, and in correspondence with the general public the use of Italian should be as much as possible discouraged. The records of the Council of Government and its Select Committees should also be kept in English alone. By this means much labour now spent in translation would be avoided.

27. Many letters and papers received in this office, which are of little or no importance and not at all likely to be required for reference, now lumber the Registry and occupy the time of the registering clerk. It will be sufficient to file such documents without registration.

28. Instead of entering in the manuscript letter books all local letters outwards, numbering some two thousand a year, impressions of such letters should be taken by a copying-press.

29. The calculations and reports necessary to determine the several rates of pension to be assigned to Civil Servants, now performed by Clerk No. 1, as well as the preparation of Quarterly Returns of the changes in the Establishments, for transmission to the Colonial Office, and the collection from the various branches of requisitions for the ordinary monthly expenditure, should be transferred to other Departments.* The Chief Secretary's Office. Miscellaneous Returns. * See par. 279.

30. I also propose that the issuing of Passports, of all Warrants to act as advocates, legal procurators, notaries, physicians, surgeons, land surveyors, &c., and of all Licences to act as auctioneers, to deal in marine stores, and to carry on various other occupations, as well as the performance on behalf of the Governor of the duties of Registrar under the Merchant Shipping Act of 1854, which are now entrusted to the Chief Secretary's Office, be removed elsewhere.† Passports, Licences, &c. † See paras. 66 and 126.

31. These changes will in my opinion, notwithstanding the proposal which I shall make to transfer to it the control of the Government printing business and the supply of stationery to the various Departments,‡ fully justify the reduction in the Chief Secretary's Office of at least one Senior Clerk. Proposed saving in the Establishment. ‡ See par. 200.

THE TREASURY.

32. This Department consists of a Cashier, three Clerks and two Messengers, and is maintained at an estimated cost of £921 a year. The Treasury.

33. The Cashier's chief duty is to receive all monies accruing to the Government, and to pay all its liabilities, retaining for daily use about £4000 or £5000, and placing the remainder, averaging about £50,000, in a reserve chest, under the joint custody of three persons, of whom he is one. He is also nominally the only Government accountant in the Island, embodying, and rendering monthly to the Auditor-General, abstracts of the sums received and paid by the Heads of all other public Departments, who are his sub-accountants. Business of the Department.

34. The average balance in both the Treasury chests on the 15th and 30th of every month during the past ten years has been about £55,000, the amount being sometimes as high as £80,000, while the lowest on any one of those dates, due only to exceptional circumstances, has exceeded £25,000. This money has been totally unproductive in the hands of the Government. Except under special conditions, as in the case of important works entered upon after being voted in Council, and the requirements of which can be long foreseen, the weekly receipts are fully equal to the weekly payments, and consequently a very small reserve is sufficient for carrying on the business of the Government. I consider that no more than £10,000 should, as a rule, be kept in the Treasury chests, and that the rest should be invested in Consols, which, assuming the average balance so dealt with to be no more than £45,000, would yield interest amounting, at the rate of 3 per cent., to upwards of £1350 a year. Should the local cash balance require at any time to be suddenly expanded to provide for extraordinary expenditure, this can be done by disposing of bills drawn on the reserve fund represented by Consols. Proposed Investment of the Redundant Balances

35. A convenient modification of that suggestion, and one more in harmony with the arrangements in other colonies, would be the transference of the banking business now done by the Treasury to one or both of the local Banks. During my visit to Malta I was in communication with the Presidents and Directors of these establishments, the Bank of Malta and the Anglo-Maltese Bank, on this subject. Our correspondence has not yet led to acceptable proposals, but I still think that satisfactory terms may be agreed upon; or, failing that, it is probable that a suitable arrangement may be made with one of the English Banks having branches in the East, by which the Government will be relieved of the responsibility of acting as its own banker. Proposed Employment of the Local Banks.

36. On this point I am unable at present to speak definitively. In either case, however, it appears to me unnecessary to maintain the Treasury as a separate establishment. The business of the office is conducted with extreme care and regularity, highly creditable to those who are responsible for carrying out the system at present in force. But its labours are so light that I am of opinion they can be easily and satisfactorily performed, with great advantage to the public service, by being merged with the duties now assigned to the Land Revenue Department, for which I shall propose, in the following section of this Report, to make fresh provision.§ I therefore recommend that the Department of the Treasury, as now constituted, be abolished. Proposal to abolish the Treasury. § See par. 64.

37. The Cashier has reached an age at which, I presume, he will be glad to avail himself of the retirement that he has so well earned by his lengthened service under Savings to be thus effected.

THE LAND REVENUE AND PUBLIC WORKS DEPARTMENT.

The Treasury. consider, will be sufficient for the work to be transferred, even if no arrangement should be made with the local Banks. In the latter case the entire present strength of the Treasury can be dispensed with. Thus, in addition to the proceeds of the investment of the redundant balances, an ultimate saving of from £700 to £900 per annum may be looked for.

Land Revenue and Public Works Department.
38. With an establishment consisting of a Collector and a Deputy Collector, five Clerks, five Surveyors, a Clerk of Works, three Draughtsmen, and about thirty other subordinates, the estimated cost of this Department is £3740 a year, while the money collected by it from all sources in 1877 was about £43,186, and its expenditure on works, buildings, roads, and streets, amounted to £44,752. As a Revenue Department it is second only to the Customs in importance, and it is responsible for the spending of more than twice as much money as any other branch of the public service in Malta.

Defects and Abuses in its Management.
39. The clerical duties of the Department appear to be, in almost every particular, efficiently performed. Its past management, however, has, I regret to say, been so faulty, and its present condition is so unsatisfactory, that nothing but a complete reconstruction can bring it into such a state of efficiency as the interests of the Government imperatively demand. In justification of this remark and of the changes which I shall propose, it is necessary that I should point out some of the more prominent defects and abuses which have come under my notice, and the knowledge of which has given rise to an exaggerated impression on the public mind that they are the result of favouritism and culpable neglect, if not of corruption.

40. The chief cause of this unfortunate state of things appears to be in the fact that the duties and responsibilities imposed on the Head of the Department are more than a person of ordinary intelligence and capacity should be expected to perform properly. He is entrusted with greater power than he can safely exercise, and there is little more than a theoretical control over his actions. His primary functions being those of Collector of Land Revenue, he is under constant temptation to subordinate them to the pressing claims made upon him as Superintendent of Public Works; and as he rarely has the professional knowledge necessary for the adequate performance of the latter, both branches of his business are liable to become disorganised.

41. It would appear, indeed, that there never has been any satisfactory organisation for levying the full amount of land revenue to which the Government has a right. The large estates formerly possessed by the Knights of St. John, and which fell to the Crown * See Appendix B. when Malta was ceded to Great Britain,* were at first applied especially to Imperial purposes. So much of them as is required for the defence of the Island or for the residence of the troops, is in fact still retained by the military authorities, the other portions having been assigned to the Local Government to aid in defraying the public expenses of the Colony. From the first, however, much of this property was misapplied by granting it, without charge or at greatly reduced rents, to Government employés and others who had influence enough to obtain in this way illicit and indirect pensions. Thus the notion has been allowed to prevail that Government lands and houses differ from other property, that admission to tenancy of them is a matter of favour, and that tenants, once accepted, have a claim to special indulgences as regards not only abatement of rent and payment of rent in arrear, but also licence to allow the property to fall out of repair, or, if they maintain it in good order, to make a profit by sub-letting or transferring their leases to other parties.

Neglect of Regulations as regards Surveys and Repairs.
42. The economical management of the public property necessarily depends, in large measure, on the zeal and honesty with which it is looked after, under the supervision of the Collector, by the Surveyors, or Periti, as they are styled in Malta. Regulations intended to secure this object have been laid down by the Government, but in the most important points they have been largely disregarded. Thus, in the covenant for an eight years' lease of urban property, it is clearly stipulated that the tenant is to execute all ordinary repairs, and this stipulation is of course taken account of in determining the amount of rent to be paid. So lax has been the management, however, that the covenants, though signed, are never enforced, and, although in a few of the better class of houses, repairs are from time to time voluntarily executed by the tenants, the great bulk of the property is allowed to deteriorate until the Government is finally obliged to incur heavy expenditure in itself effecting the tenants' repairs. It appears that during the past five years more than 11 per cent. of the amount of rent received has on an average, been expended in repairs to the rented property, which, being nearly all let on repairing leases, ought I apprehend, certainly not to cost more than 1 or 2

per cent. It is alleged in the Department that the failure of the Government to compel tenants to execute the repairs for which they are responsible, is partly caused by its own neglect in executing such other repairs as it is itself liable for. But if this is really the case, it only aggravates the complaint that may justly be made as to the mismanagement of public affairs.

LAND RE-
VENUE AND
PUBLIC
WORKS
DEPARTMENT.

43. Again, in a Code of Instructions prepared in 1858 for the guidance of the Collector, it is provided that on the expiration of a lease which contains no provision to the contrary, if the tenement is not put up to public competition, and the former tenant desires to renew his lease, a fresh valuation, in order to determine the amount of rent to be paid, shall be "made by two Land Surveyors of the Department, separately from and independently of each other, each of whom is to specify in a written report the grounds of his valuation." Such double valuations, I have reason to believe, are hardly ever made. Where a lease has to be renewed, its survey or inspection, if done at all, is generally a mere matter of form, assigned to one Perito who, except in a few rare cases, furnishes no report of his proceedings, and no record is kept in the office to show the grounds on which the value of the tenement was arrived at. It is impossible to say to what extent the public revenue has suffered from this neglect of regulations; but there can be no doubt that Government property is very frequently sublet by its tenants with such advantage to themselves as would be impossible if the valuations by the Periti were properly made. In proof of this I give the following instances, which have been brought to my notice, and the accuracy of which I have ascertained by personal inquiry and inspection of the documents referring to them.

Incorrect Valuations.

44. (1.) A.B. held the lease of a building which expired on the 31st of December, 1877, and in accordance with which a rental of £105 a year had been paid. Availing himself of his legal right, he applied for a renewal of his lease, and a single Perito was sent to re-value the building. It was known that the lessee was receiving £211 16s. 8d. in rents for portions of the property which he had sub-let. In spite of that, however, the whole was re-valued at only £122, and at that slightly increased rental a fresh lease was granted to him, so that he is now realising a net income of £89 16s. 8d. from the house, besides retaining a part, rent-free, for his own residence.

45. (2.) In August 1871, the "fixtures, goodwill, and right of tenancy" of a shop which C.D. had leased from the Government at a rental of £36 a year, was disposed of by him to E.F. for £400, to be paid in four annual instalments, it being further stipulated that C.D. was to give his consent to E.F.'s being recognised by the Government as tenant in his stead. The "fixtures," from the nature of C.D.'s trade, cannot have been of much value, and, as E.F. was precluded by the agreement from carrying on the same trade, the "goodwill" can only have been nominal. Nearly the whole of the £400, therefore, must have been for the "right of tenancy," so that, as the lease had only four years to run, E.F. really paid little short of £100 a year to C.D., in addition to the £36 a year paid to the Government, for permission to occupy a tenement that the Land Revenue Department had valued, and continued to value when it renewed the lease in July 1875, at only £36 a year. Had the shop, on the expiration of the lease, been properly valued, or had it been offered to public competition, there can be no doubt that a very much higher rental would have been obtained.

46. (3.) In October 1870, G.H. procured from I.J. the "right of tenancy and goodwill" of a shop for which the latter was paying £24 a year on an eight years' lease expiring in June 1875, on condition, if the lease was renewed, that he should pay him during the remainder of his life a pension of £7 10s. a quarter, and, if the lease was not renewed in June 1875, that from that date the pension should be reduced to £5 12s. 6d. a quarter. Here again, as the trade to be carried on by G.H. was an altogether different one to that of I.J., the "goodwill" was of no value, and G.H., whose application for a renewal of the lease on the same terms as before was acceded to by the Land Revenue Department, has been paying, until a few months ago—when, as I am informed, I.J. died—an actual rental of £54 a year, of which the Government has been content to receive four-ninths, leaving the other five-ninths to be appropriated by I.J. in consideration of his surrendering a tenement which the Government had allowed him during many years to occupy for less than half of what it was presumably worth.

47. In cases like the above, had the rules laid down for the guidance of the Department in such matters been complied with—that is, had the reports of two professional men, acting independently of each other, been submitted to the consideration of a competent authority,—it is scarcely possible to conceive that the leases would have been renewed at such low rents as are now paid.

48. I find, moreover, that long leases, for terms varying from fifty to ninty-nine years, are frequently granted without competition at very low rents, ostensibly on the ground

LAND REVENUE AND PUBLIC WORKS DEPARTMENT.

Unfulfilled Contracts for Improvements.

that in each case the tenant is to incur considerable expenditure, often a specified sum, in adding to or improving the property, but that, although this expenditure is as much a part of the consideration money as the rent itself, steps are not taken by the Department to see that the stipulated amount is spent, or that the promised improvements are properly effected. No record is to be found in the office showing that, after the execution of such leases, any attempt is made to enforce them. In fact, the evidence of the Department itself goes to prove that no subsequent surveys or reports are ever made with this object, and that as regards all such conditions the leases are little better than waste paper.

Partiality in letting Property.

49. The rule that vacant tenements are to be let by public competition—which is held not to apply to extensions of leases—is frequently ignored on one pretext or another, and, even when it is followed, the highest bidder is occasionally set aside in favour of a lower, on grounds which it would be difficult to justify. I have before me the case of a house, which, on the termination of an eight years' lease at £70 a year, was put up to competition in September 1877. A.B. offered £66, and C.D. offered £50 5s., while four other tenders were for lower amounts. A.B.'s offer included a proposal, "subject to Government's consent, to make sundry improvements which will render the property more valuable in the future," and he was willing to pay a year's rent in advance. On his declining, however, to give security, of a sort not usually required, for future payments, his tender was rejected in favour of C.D.'s, from whom no such security was exacted, and who was under no obligation to improve the property. Instances may, of course, occur in which the highest bidder ought not to be accepted; but no evidence is contained in the records of the office as to the existence of any valid objection in the case of A.B.

Arrears of Rents.

50. In addition to the indulgence shown to the tenants of Government property by allowing them in many cases to hold it at rentals far below the amounts that could be obtained by public competition or would be insisted upon by other proprietors, and also by ignoring the conditions of the leases with regard to repairs and improvements, there appears to have been most unjustifiable negligence in the collection of rents. A stipulation that the rent shall be paid half-yearly in advance is introduced into all leases of urban property, while those for rural property require the payment of rent in three instalments per annum, and in all cases it is provided that the leases shall become null and void if rent is not paid within ten days of its being asked for after it is due. These reasonable precautions, however, appear to have been systematically disregarded. The arrears of rents due to the Department on the 15th of December, 1877, amounted to £6017 10s. 6d. The disclosure of this state of things caused special efforts to be made towards amending it, and the arrears were, by the 1st of October, 1878, reduced to £4290 9s.; but of this amount by far the greater portion is probably now irrecoverable.

The Periti.

51. Such shortcomings as those I have called attention to are due to a want of proper organisation and supervision, especially in the Public Works branch of the Department, although the other cannot be exonerated. The Surveyors or Periti, upon whom devolve most important duties, and who are nominally under the direction of the Collector, appear in practice to be independent of all control. Whenever they absent themselves from the office it is considered sufficient for them to write "Gone to the country" against their names in the attendance-book, without making any precise statement of the grounds of their absence. Although the Collector receives a travelling allowance of £50 a year, presumably for the purpose, *inter alia*, of looking after these Surveyors, it would seem that his numerous other occupations prevent his doing so. When I add that by the terms of their engagements the Periti are allowed to carry on private practice as surveyors, such a lax mode of conducting public business will be seen to be especially undesirable.

The Best Method of dealing with Government Property.

52. In considering what improvements can be effected in the present arrangements for dealing with the Government property in lands and houses, the most difficult question that presents itself is as to the primary conditions on which that property shall be leased. Very different opinions, each more or less strongly supported, are held on the subject; but the weightiest arguments appear to me to be in favour of following, with certain modifications, the course adopted by the ecclesiastical bodies and private proprietors, who are said to divide between them in equal parts about two-thirds of the property, measured by its value, though more than two-thirds in extent, and who, doubtless with more regard to their respective financial interests than the Government is likely to feel, show a marked preference for short leases, the chief difference being that the former throw minor repairs upon the tenants, and that the latter execute them themselves.

53. Were such a course expedient or even practicable, the simplest and most certain

way of handling the subject would undoubtedly be that suggested by Mr. Rowsell; viz., to sell the property and invest the sum realised in Consols. I do not think, however, that it would be either one or the other. As the great landlord of the Colony, the Government secures an influence which is not without its advantages at present, and which may be far more important in the future. The chief drawback to those advantages lies in the inconvenience and difficulty of maintaining a Department to administer the property, which is almost inevitably more costly in public than in private hands. As the only way of disposing of the Crown lands and houses, however, without submitting to a great sacrifice, and without depreciating all real property to an extent that would be equivalent to a heavy tax upon other owners, and might prove ruinous to them, would be to sell it by driblets, the administrative department would have to be continued for an indefinite period, and the contemplated saving would be too remote to be of any appreciable value. Not only would the measure be a very unpopular one, moreover, but it might happen, in a moment of extravagance or of financial pressure, that the capital would be made away with. [*LAND REVENUE AND PUBLIC WORKS DEPARTMENT. Objections to Sale of the Property.*]

54. The alternative of perpetual leases, advocated by some persons, is, in my opinion, open to as strong objections. To extend the process to all Government property would require considerable time, and, when so extended, almost as much supervision as is now called for would have to be exercised in order to prevent the property from reverting to the Government, through non-fulfilment of covenants, in a comparatively worthless condition, and in all probability after tedious and expensive legal proceedings had been incurred. [*Perpetual Leases.*]

55. For these reasons I cannot recommend that, as a rule, Government property should be either sold or let on perpetual lease.

56. Long leases may be proper in certain cases, where barren land is to be reclaimed, or where new buildings are to be erected by tenants, but the terms on which every such lease is to be granted should be made the subject of special consideration and report by a properly-constituted authority. [*Long Leases.*]

57. With such exceptions as that authority may sanction, which might reasonably include all lands and tenements the rent of which is less than £5 per annum, I think it will be found advantageous to the Government, and not unfair to tenants, to let all urban and rural property, subject to the existing conditions as to repairs, &c., for periods of not more than four years, with option to the tenant to renew for four years more upon satisfactory evidence being produced that the terms of his lease, as regards payment of rent and execution of repairs, have been complied with. At the end of every eighth year the property should be re-valued by at least two Periti named by the Government, and acting separately and independently of each other. On the valuation thus arrived at, the tenant in possession, provided the conditions of his former lease have been satisfactorily fulfilled, should have the option of obtaining a new lease for the same period as before, i.e., four years, with liberty to extend it to eight. [*Short Leases. Re-valuations on Renewal.*]

58. Relinquished or vacant lands and tenements should invariably be put up to public competition, and, subject to the offer being above a certain limit to be fixed by the proper authority beforehand, be assigned to the highest eligible bidder. [*Public Competition.*]

59. The present rules as to the periods at which rents are to be paid—every six months in advance in the case of urban property, and thrice a year in arrear in the case of rural property—may very properly be maintained; but care should be taken that they are enforced, instead of being treated as dead letters. [*Prompt Payment of Rents.*]

60. The sub-letting of Government property, in whole or in part, should be forbidden, unless the details have been reported to the authorities and their consent has been obtained. [*Sub-letting.*]

61. The policy hitherto pursued by the Land Revenue Department of abstaining from doing anything calculated to raise the rents of Government property, on the ground that such a measure would result in a proportionate increase in the rates now charged by the ecclesiastical bodies and by private owners, does not appear to me to be based on sound principles. Though it may be the duty of the Government, within certain limits, to act the part of a generous landlord, it is no less bound in the interests of the community at large and as the steward of the public estate, to turn that estate to the best possible account by insuring the full market price for that which it has to dispose of. That it should place its rents on a par with those of other proprietors, appears to me, therefore, not only a perfectly legitimate proceeding, but one which it is bound to adopt, and I shall be greatly surprised if a careful administration of the Government lands and buildings in Malta, on the principles which I have indicated, does not result, so soon as those principles can be brought to bear upon the whole property, in an addition of at least £6000 a year to the revenue. [*Increased Rentals.*]

LAND RE-VENUE AND PUBLIC WORKS DEPARTMENT.	62. To secure this and the other advantages that ought to be looked for, however, I consider it necessary that the departmental arrangements for conducting the duties connected with the Land Revenue and Public Works should be entirely reconstructed, and
Proposed Departmental Reforms.	as a first step towards this end, it appears to me imperative that these duties should be distributed among separate branches of the public service. It is with considerable reluctance that I recommend this course; but I see no other way of removing the obstacles that present themselves. The director of such an office as the Land Revenue and Public Works Department was doubtless intended to be, when it was constituted in 1859, should possess administrative, financial and professional talents which, I fear, it would be hopeless to look for in any single member of the Civil Service of Malta at the present moment; and the importance of his being thoroughly conversant with the languages of the Island, if no other objections existed, would deter me from suggesting that the chief of such a Department should be sought for out of the Colony. The only alternative, therefore, is to subdivide and adapt the work to the officials to whom it has to be entrusted; and as to the expediency of this course I am glad to know that I am in some measure supported by the opinions expressed by His Excellency the Governor, in his confidential despatch to you of the 14th of August last.
Proposed separation of the Land Revenue and Public Works Departments.	63. I accordingly propose that the Public Works be separated from the Land Revenue branch, and that to an officer who might be properly styled a Director, be transferred from both branches all duties connected with contracts, whether as regards the letting or selling of property, the procuring of supplies, or the making of contracts for public works.
RECEIVER-GENERAL'S DEPARTMENT.	64. The Revenue branch would thus be converted into a purely financial Department, over which I would place an officer to be called a Receiver-General, who should be charged also with the duties at present performed by the Treasury, which Department should henceforth disappear.*
* See par. 36. To perform Land Revenue duties.	65. The Receiver-General's Department, in accordance with this proposal, would not only collect the rents of lands and houses, the proceeds of the sale of lands and of water-supply, and the miscellaneous credits now accounted for by the Land Revenue
To absorb the Treasury.	Department, but would also receive the collections of all other Departments, as the Treasury now does. It would make all the payments at present made by the latter Department, and would become the only direct accountant with the Auditor-General. All other Departments and Establishments now acting as sub-accountants with the Cashier would occupy exactly the same position towards the Receiver-General.
To issue Licences.	66. The issuing of all licences, or other instruments for which money is paid—except those connected with the Customs and the Port Departments, which might more
† See par. 122.	conveniently be furnished at the water-side†—should, moreover, devolve on the Receiver-General's Department, such documents as it is not competent to the Receiver-General himself to authorise being prepared on the certificates of the several Heads of Depart-
‡ See par. 30.	ments concerned.‡
Proposed Staff of the Receiver-General's Department.	67. The Receiver-General should, I consider, draw the salary of £500 a year now assigned to the Collector of Land Revenue, but have no allowance for transport, as his duties will not often require him to travel. If, besides the Deputy Receiver and the Summoning Messenger at Gozo, he retain from his present establishment three Clerks, one Office Messenger, and four Summoning and Country Messengers, and there be added to them two out of the three Clerks, the Messenger and the Money Porter taken from the Treasury, he will have a very strong staff with which to establish his new Department in thorough working order, and will be able to dispense with the supernumeraries as vacancies occur in his own or other offices. I am of opinion that, when it is duly organised, four Clerks and six Messengers and Porters will amply suffice for the work that will have to be done by the Receiver-General's Department. Should the contemplated arrangement with the local Banks be adopted, at least another Clerk and another Messenger may, I consider, be dispensed with.
PUBLIC WORKS DEPARTMENT.	68. The Works branch, to which I propose to give a separate and independent existence, assigning to it a secondary position in the rank of Departments, should have at its head a professional man, who would be precluded from private practice and required to devote his whole time to the business of his office, and who might be designated Superintendent of Works.
Outline of its Duties.	69. This Department should be charged with the custody and structural maintenance of all buildings and property belonging to the Government, and be held responsible for the proper upkeep of all public Roads, Aqueducts and Gardens, including the Addolorata Cemetery. All new works, and even repairs of any magnitude, should be executed by contract, and the principal duties of the professional staff should be limited to the preparation of data upon which contracts could be formed, to supervising the

execution of such contracts, to making periodical and special surveys and valuations PUBLIC WORKS DEPARTMENT. affecting rents and repairs, and to executing by hired labour such minor repairs and services as could not well be made subjects of contract.

70. In no case should entering into contracts for the sale or lease of property devolve upon the Receiver-General's Department, nor should contracts of any kind be entered into by the Public Works Department. These services will be provided for elsewhere, to the great relief, in labour and individual responsibility, of the heads of both these sections of the public service. *Contracts and Leases.*

71. The peculiar relations in which the Government of Malta stands towards the people as regards the custody and construction of public buildings and other property will inevitably render the functions of the Public Works Department in this, as compared with other colonies, disproportionately large and important. Not only has the Government to perform many duties which elsewhere generally fall upon the municipal authorities, but there are also assigned to it various tasks and responsibilities, which, in other portions of the British Empire, it is found expedient to leave in private hands, or under the care of independent corporations. *Importance of the Public Works Department.*

72. The Opera House furnishes the most remarkable illustration of this state of things. Exaggerated statements as to the cost of the building are often put forward by adverse critics, but the actual expenditure on its original construction, decoration and furnishing, including £10,272, the value of the site occupied by it, is shown in the accounts of the Land Revenue Department to have amounted to as much as £51,486, while the expenses of restoration after the disastrous fire of the 25th of May, 1873, exceeded £12,000. Besides the rent, £250 a year, charged to the present lessee, the shops attached to the theatre now yield £62 6s. a year. This total of £312 6s., however, hardly does more than cover the incidental expenses of maintenance, including the allowance made to the Clerk of Works as custodian of the building, and the cost of the policemen in attendance during the performances, even if no account be taken of the services of some members of the Government whose duty it is to see that the performances are conducted in a satisfactory manner. *The Opera House.*

73. A more profitable speculation of the Government is the Valletta Market, erected between 1858 and 1862 at an expense of £17,980 7s. 6d., and now maintained at an average cost of about £109 a year. As the rental obtained in 1877 for stalls and cellars amounted to £2408 10s. 9d., it would seem that about 12¾ per cent. on the capital expended is annually credited to the public as a set-off against interest and deterioration. *The Valletta Market.*

74. The formation of the Addolorata Cemetery, which was begun in 1862 and opened in 1869, was probably, in the interests of public health, a necessary duty devolving upon the Government in the absence of any other local organization by which it could be taken in hand. It seems only reasonable, however, that it should be made, in part at any rate, self-supporting, as are similar institutions elsewhere. This is not attempted. The expenses of its formation, and the supplementary charges incurred up to October 1878, amount to £31,735 4s. 7d. During that period £1004 8s. 10d. has been realised by the sale of sites and graves, and this is the only credit appearing in the accounts of the Land Revenue Department. A charge of £4 for a grave is in some cases made, but in accordance with an Ordinance passed in 1869, graves have been assigned gratuitously to all persons applying for them who previously had the right of burial in certain churches. The payment for a grave, moreover, appears to entitle its possessor and his successors to have it opened and closed, and to obtain all the services incidental to funerals, as often as may be necessary, in perpetuity, at the Government expense, instead of, as formerly, having to pay for them themselves. In addition to an allowance of £35 to the Medical Inspector, the Land Revenue Department is charged with the wages of a head guardian, eight guardians and grave-diggers, and a gate-keeper, amounting to £330 a year; while the charges for ecclesiastical services, including the salaries of a Capuchin friar and a lay brother, the travelling expenses of parish priests attending the burials of paupers, and other items, amount to £305 10s. a year. Most of these charges appear only to have been found necessary since the Government showed itself willing to defray them. Even if it is considered proper that in connection with paupers' funerals ecclesiastical expenses not formerly incurred should now be admitted as a small indirect subsidy to the Church, every one above the rank of a pauper ought surely to be held responsible for all the expenses connected with the use, from time to time, of the grave owned by him. That is the method pursued in connection with the cemetery known as "Ta Braxia," which is used by Protestants and others who are not Roman Catholics. *The Addolorata Cemetery.*

75. Besides the joint-Cathedral Church of San Giovanni in Valletta, the Government

14

PUBLIC WORKS DEPARTMENT.

Churches and Chapels.
* See Appendix B. (III.)

has inherited from the Knights of St. John several other Roman Catholic Churches and Chapels in various parts of Malta, which, however, entail on it only responsibility and expense.* Between 1867 and 1875, a special outlay of £5886 8s. 5d. was incurred in restoring the painted ceiling of the Church of San Giovanni, re-gilding it, renewing its monuments and repairing the churchyard wall, while the ordinary expenditure on account of all these churches and chapels, based on an average of the past seven years, is £604 8s. 1d. per annum. In addition to structural repairs, the charges include all sorts of miscellaneous items, such as "silvering candlesticks," "cleaning sacred utensils," and "providing sacred vestments." As to the propriety of charging such expenses against the public revenue, I offer no opinion, but so long as that is done, it would certainly seem right that the protection of all ecclesiastical furniture of this description should devolve upon the Government, and that those to whom it is entrusted should be held responsible for its safe custody and use only in legitimate ways.

Furniture and other movable Property.

76. I find that no inventory is kept either of such Church furniture or, with one or two exceptions, of the fixtures and movable property in the several offices occupied by the various Departments. Rough memoranda, purporting to be lists of the furniture and pictures belonging to the public in the Governor's three palaces, have been prepared on two or three occasions, but these are manifestly incomplete—the valuable relics contained in the armoury, for example, being omitted—and altogether untrustworthy. A careful inventory of all the furniture and other property in the palaces should be prepared and preserved in the Public Works Department, all additions and replacements being duly noted in it from time to time, to be verified before the close of each Governor's departure, in order that his successor may know exactly what property is placed at his disposal and will have to be surrendered by him on his leaving the Island. Similar inventories should be kept for each of the public offices and for every Government Church, and these inventories should be checked by periodical surveys, the several custodians being held accountable by the Public Works Department for all deficiencies and deteriorations that cannot be satisfactorily explained. For each building or Department a Property Book should be kept in which all new furniture should be entered, and every deduction noted and explained.

77. While the protection and maintenance of the contents of all such buildings, as well as of the buildings themselves, ought to devolve upon the Public Works Department, the expenses incurred in connection with them ought to be separated, and assigned in the public accounts to the several Departments and Establishments concerned.

The Public Gardens.
† See par. 18.

78. I have already suggested a plan for the more profitable treatment of the Gardens at Sant' Antonio and Boschetto.†

Proposed Staff of the Public Works Department.

79. The permanent staff of the Public Works Department should be confined within the narrowest possible limits. I consider that £300 a year will be a sufficient salary for the Superintendent, and that—exclusive of the Periti—two Clerks, a Clerk of Works and Assistant, two Draughtsmen, and a Messenger, will suffice for the indoor duties of his establishment. The Overseers of Masons, Carpenters, and others, the Superintendent of Public Gardens, the Guardians of Aqueducts, and the Head Guardian of the Addolorata Cemetery, may perhaps with propriety continue to be permanent employés, entitled to pension; but all other subordinates, whether gardeners, watchmen, grave-diggers, gate-keepers, or labourers, should, as the present men retire, cease to have a claim on the Government for life-long employment and superannuation.

80. Some confusion might be avoided if the Clerk of Works, who now draws £75 a year for his services in the Land Revenue Department, £65 for services connected with the lighting of the streets, and £60 as custodian of the Opera House, were to receive his salary of £200 for general service under the Superintendent of Works. On the other hand the accounts of this Department should be relieved of the charge of £35 paid to the Chief Police Physician for acting as Medical Inspector of Addolorata Cemetery, and the amount, so long as it is paid, should be included with the other items by which that functionary is remunerated.‡

‡ See par. 180.

81. Whether the Periti in Government employ should be salaried officers proper, or should, like professional men in private life, be paid solely by fees for the work performed by them, I leave to be decided by the local authorities when vacancies occur in the present staff; but the system of allowing them to engage in private practice while they are permanent officials having a right to superannuation, should, I consider, be discontinued as soon as possible; and, in any case, they should be required to make all valuations and survey and progress reports in detail and in writing. Instead of being allowed to draw a specified sum annually in lieu of travelling expenses, moreover, they should be recouped, subject to the approval of the proper authority, for the actual and necessary expenses incurred by them.

82. It should be the duty of the Superintendent to pay frequent visits to works and buildings, and to make himself acquainted with the manner in which his subordinates perform their several functions. For this purpose he should, like the Periti, be provided with travelling accommodation at the public expense. Public Works Department.

83. In relieving the two branches of the Land Revenue and Public Works Department from administrative responsibility with regard to letting or selling the public property, and from the labour connected with contracts on public works, it becomes necessary to make other provision for dealing with these important affairs. What is wanted is such improved machinery as, without unnecessarily adding to the expense of management, and if possible with direct economy, will at the same time be effective in operation, and calculated to secure public confidence. After the most anxious consideration, I am satisfied that this may best be done by placing it beyond the power of any one person to influence any sale, lease, or contract of any kind. Proposed Arrangements for Contracts and Leases.

84. These highly responsible duties I therefore propose to entrust to a Director of Contracts, aided by not fewer than two heads of Departments, who, with him as Chairman, shall form a Committee, empowered to deal with all such matters. This Committee may most properly be formed of the Director of Contracts, the Collector of Customs, and the Receiver-General, substituting for one of the two last named either the Controller of Charitable Institutions, the Superintendent of Works, or the Superintendent of the Ports, whenever the matters to be dealt with more especially concern their respective Departments. Thus it would always fall to the lot of the first three to dispose of questions relating to the sale or lease of property, and to two of the former and one of the supplementary members to deal with contracts for works or supplies. The initiative in all the business to be done by the Committee should devolve on the Director. Contract Committee.

85. For an extension or renewal of lease the following documents would be required: (1) Application from the tenant in possession, endorsed by the Receiver-General with a Report as to the punctuality observed in the payment of rent; (2) Reports from the Periti confirmed by the Superintendent of Works, as to the condition of the property, and, when necessary, the rental value and estimated cost of repairs. For re-letting or selling relinquished lands or tenements, the latter Reports only would be necessary. It would be the duty of the Director to procure these documents, to lay them before the Committee and obtain its written recommendations thereon, and to submit these recommendations to His Excellency the Governor, through the usual channel, for his decision. Should the decision be in favour of renewal or extension, the Director would then instruct the Government Notary to complete the contract in the customary manner. Should it be in favour of offering the property to public competition, it would be the duty of the Director to advertise for tenders, to open in the presence of the Committee such as might be received, and to follow out the Committee's recommendations as in the case of renewed or extended leases. The Letting or Selling of Government Lands and Houses.

86. For new buildings or works of considerable magnitude, designs, specifications and estimates should either be furnished to the Director by the Superintendent of Works or be obtained by public competition. In either case the principle should be strictly preserved of making the Contract Committee responsible for the selection of the contractors. Contracts for New Works or Buildings.

87. Periodical contracts for the maintenance of roads, land transport, supplies of provisions, materials, and articles of every kind required for the public service, should be dealt with in the same manner by the Director and the Committee, the heads of the several Departments furnishing to the Director all such specifications and information as contractors may reasonably require, and as can leave no doubt as to the nature and quality of the articles to be supplied or the work to be done. Instead of each Department making its own contract as at present, one contract for the same article or class of article would suffice for the whole service. By this arrangement the number of contracts entered into on account of the public would be far fewer than at present, clerical labour in dealing with them would be lessened, better and more uniform quality would be ensured, and contractors of a superior class to those now frequently to be found would probably become purveyors to the Government. At the same time it would be the duty of the Committee to see that no single contractor was allowed to monopolise undertakings, as for the upkeep of too great a mileage of roads, which there was not a reasonable prospect of his being able satisfactorily to perform. Contracts for Roads, Provisions, Stores, &c.

88. In short, all contracts of whatever kind should be entered into under the responsibility of the Contract Committee, acting through the Director. It should be the duty of the latter to see that the Head of each Department is supplied with copies of all contracts in which he is concerned; and it should be the duty of every such head Relation of the Contract Committee and Receiver-General's Department with other Departments.

CONTRACT COMMITTEE.
to furnish from time to time certificates, which would form the basis of the contractor's claim on the Receiver-General for payment, as to the amounts due on account of supplies furnished to or work performed for his Department.

Relations of the Public Works Department with other Departments.
89. The various Heads of Departments, lessees of Government property, and other individuals requiring the services of the Public Works Department, should obtain them by direct written application to its Superintendent, who, if such requests appear to him legitimate and proper, should prepare specifications, estimates, &c., for the work to be done, and forward them to the Director of Contracts, in order, if the proposal is sanctioned, that, according to the nature and magnitude of the work, public tenders may be called for, or permission may be given to proceed to the execution of it by hired labour.

90. On the other hand, when valuations of houses or lands shall become necessary, with a view to selling or letting such property without competition, the Director of Contracts should instruct the Superintendent of Works to cause surveys and estimates to be made by the Periti, and their written reports should be sent to the Director and be recorded only in his office.

Surveys and Repairs, &c.
91. The Public Works Department should also be held responsible for the due fulfilment of all covenants of leases which impose upon tenants the liability of keeping their tenements in repair. To secure this important end, occasional surveys of all Government property should be made, and the Surveyors' reports should be regularly transmitted to the Director of Contracts.

Meetings of the Contract Committee.
92. I consider that a meeting of the Contract Committee once a week will suffice for all the business likely to come before it, if that business is carefully prepared by the Director; and I propose, for reasons which will be stated in a subsequent part of this Report, that the Auditor-General for the time being shall be *ex officio* Director of Contracts.*

See par. 275.

Advantages of the Proposed Changes.
93. The system thus sketched out is not a new one. It has been successfully adopted under other Governments, and I see no reason why it should not work well in Malta. It has at any rate the merit of affording a better guarantee for a sound administration of the public property than now exists, and of reducing within the compass of an ordinary capacity the labours that cause lamentable and mischievous embarrassment to the present Department of Land Revenue and Public Works.

94. I am unable to estimate accurately the economies that ought to result from the proposed arrangements when they are in working order. But I believe that, besides the small reductions in work and responsibility that will be effected in the Charitable Institutions and other Departments which will be relieved of the duty of making contracts, the whole establishment transferred from the Treasury, with the exception of one clerk, can be dispensed with and the work be efficiently done, especially if copying-presses be used, with the addition of only one to the number of employés now in the Land Revenue and Public Works and the Audit Departments.

THE CUSTOMS DEPARTMENT.

The Customs Department.
95. About two-thirds of the entire revenue of Malta, and three times as much as is derived from any other source, are collected by the Customs Department. Its important duties are performed by a Collector, with a salary of £500 a year, seven Clerks, receiving in all £715 a year, a Head Storekeeper, five Assistant Storekeepers, six Overseers of Deliveries, and five Guardians of Stores, receiving in all £1050, a Gauger at £110 and an Assistant Gauger at £80, a Superintendent of Weighers receiving £45 a year and fees, twenty-eight Extra Overseers and two Messengers receiving £776 a year, and about a hundred and twenty Weighers, Measurers and other subordinates who are paid by fees obtained from the trade.

Its Present Staff.

96. The work of the Department demands the exercise of great watchfulness and tact, coupled with firmness and rigid observance of discipline, so as to satisfy the commercial body and at the same time protect and maintain the revenue. The manner in which it is at present administered, the systematic organisation of all its various branches, and the energy and intelligence applied to the working-out of all its details, are highly creditable to the Collector and his staff, and leave me little to recommend in the way of further improvement or economy. All that I feel called upon to do, indeed, is to direct attention to certain points in respect of which it appears to me that the powers of the Collector may be extended or amplified with advantage.

97. Much unnecessary labour is thrown upon the Department from the manner in which merchants and traders are allowed to pass entries for dutiable goods brought into the port. In the case of a cargo of wheat intended for consumption in the Island, for instance, the importer is practically a retail dealer, without store or warehouse, and without any intention of himself paying the import duty or clearing the cargo at the Custom House. The wheat is accordingly discharged from the vessel into pontoons or lighters, for the use of which of course a charge is made by the owners, and from them, if there is room, transferred into the Corn Arcades which are Government property, and for the use of which no charge is made. From these arcades, if he is fortunate enough to gain access to them, or from the lighters, so long as the weather permits and the charge is not greater than that for landing and storing, he distributes, in small quantities, so much of the grain as he can sell to the millers or bakers, imposing upon each purchaser the obligation of passing a Customs entry for his own portion. By this process I find, in a specimen case the particulars of which are before me, that as many as 93 separate entries are made for 515 salms or quarters, being only one-third of the entire cargo of 1545 salms. When it becomes necessary to land the remainder of the cargo, it is deposited in a bonded warehouse, from which it is disposed of by the same retail process. Supposing the average quantity of each sale to be about the same—and it appears that in many instances it is even smaller—there are thus no fewer than 279 Customs entries for one cargo of 1545 salms. Some of these entries are for quantities measuring less than one salm apiece, and the great majority are for quantities on which the duty does not exceed 40s., thus enabling the person passing the entry to avoid the necessity of paying in gold, which bears a small *agio* in the market. The multiplication of these operations, each of which has to be separately recorded in the various books of the office, and the consequent receipt of innumerable small coins, not only throw much additional risk and labour on the staff of the Department, but also lead to further inconvenience, as the passing of Customs entries for such small quantities of wheat is generally assigned to a class of persons who have not intelligence or experience enabling them to perform the work without assistance from the Custom House officials, to the loss of much valuable time and the great confusion of business. The Customs Establishment is in effect turned into a sort of retail shop, with disadvantage to every one but the importer. This ought to be put a stop to, and the Collector should, in my opinion, be authorised, by law or otherwise, to suppress these practices. Entries for less than 40 salms should not be permitted, and the importers should, as in other countries, be required to employ persons competent to transact Custom House business, instead of sending messages by mere *facchini* and expecting the Government to do the work for them.

98. Similar restrictions might very properly be put on the practice of assigning to the Customs Department the task of retailing other dutiable articles to small purchasers, without compensation for the labour involved.

99. In other respects the Department ought to be fairly remunerated for services that it at present renders to the trade either gratuitously or for insufficient payment. Goods landed from vessels in the harbour, if deposited in the shed known as the Verandah, near the Custom House, on the Marina, are allowed to remain there for ten days, and even longer, without charge. This shed should be railed in and properly guarded, in the interests both of the revenue and of the owners of the goods, and a small charge should be made for the accommodation and protection afforded. I am told that agents now charge consignees and shippers 6d. for every package passing to or fro, while the Government, which provides the shed, receives nothing. I recommend that 2d. per package be charged for landing and the same for shipping, and that if the package be left for more than three days, a further charge of 6d. be made for every subsequent period of three days or less. A small cumulative fine of this sort would not only yield a slight contribution towards the expenses of the Customs Establishment, but would also expedite the passage of goods through the Verandah, and prevent a few persons from unduly monopolising the space to the exclusion of others. The same remark applies to the Corn Arcades, which have already been referred to, and to other places of temporary deposit in connection with the Custom House.

100. The charge for more regularly warehousing goods, especially cereals in bond, also needs some rectification. Seeing that the merchants are practically compelled to make use of the Government *fosse*, or granaries, the trebling of all store-rents proposed by Mr. Rowsell would be in effect an augmentation of the wheat-tax, which many are anxious now to remove or abate; but there can hardly be any objection to charging a periodical rent for the storage of cereals, as is done in the case of wine and other articles, instead of allowing a single payment to suffice for an indefinite time. At present the rent for a year, or even for many years, is no greater than that for a day. I consider that the charge of 2d. per salm now made should cover rent for only six months, and

THE CUSTOMS DEPARTMENT.

Port Dues.

that a similar amount should be claimed for every subsequent half-year or part of a half-year.

101. Without discussing the expediency of the additional harbour dues that Mr. Rowsell proposes to levy on steamers and sailing-vessels, I may say that the exemption from all Port charges accorded to sailing-vessels which enter either of the Valletta harbours in consequence of stress of weather or for repairs, provided they do not break cargo, or even if they land their cargoes for repairs, but reship them, appears to me unnecessary and unfair. These vessels enjoy all the advantages of lights, buoys, moorings, and quay accommodation, and it is only reasonable that they should contribute towards the expenses of the port as they would in any other part of the world. It would, indeed, be as proper to relieve them from the charge for pilotage as from the other dues referred to. I think that half the usual port dues, or 1½d. per ton, should be charged where no cargo is landed, and that in the case of cargoes deposited in the Verandah or goods sheds, and reshipped thence, the same charge should be made for the use of the sheds as in other cases. I do not believe that a single vessel less would enter the harbour because a trifling charge of this kind was made for essential benefits conferred. Had the proposed Port dues been levied in 1878—when, according to a Return furnished to me by the Collector of Customs, 499 sailing-ships, with an aggregate of 155,181 tons, availed themselves of the port without making any payment—the addition to the revenue would have amounted to £969 17s. 7½d.

Documents in the Italian Language.

102. While the account books of the Customs Department are all kept in the English language, permits, *cedole*, and other documents, from which entries therein are made, are written in Italian. This practice necessarily retards the clerical operations, and affords opportunities for mistakes. I am of opinion, not only that all documents emanating from the Department should be written or printed in English, but also that no document of local origin, on which the Collector is expected to take action, should be accepted from the public unless prepared in the same language.

Incomplete Manifests.

103. It should also, I consider, be insisted upon that all manifests presented to the Department be prepared in accordance with a simple form, which could easily be furnished by the Collector, separating dutiable from non-dutiable articles.

Unusual Facilities to Trade.

104. In no other port in the world, probably, are such facilities afforded by the Customs to the trade as in Valletta. With some hazard to the revenue and at considerable additional expense to the Government, steam-vessels are allowed to enter the harbour at all hours of the night, to land goods, to take in coals and cargo, to exchange passengers, and to be cleared by the Customs, so as to resume their voyage before daylight. The masters are not required, as in other places, to appear in person at the Custom House in order to enter and clear their vessels, and, instead of the production of the original manifests of the ships' cargoes being insisted upon, the consignees or agents are allowed to furnish manifests prepared by themselves. Entries of cargoes outwards are also dispensed with, in order apparently that the destination of goods intended to be smuggled into other countries may not be revealed, and consequently no official record is kept of the exports of the Colony.

105. Whether all these unusually liberal arrangements are legitimate, I am not prepared to say. As to the expediency of fostering the trade of the Port in every reasonable manner, there can be no doubt; but care should be taken in distinguishing what is from what is not necessary to that end. By far the most important trade of Malta at the present time is that of supplying steam-ships with coal, and I shall be clearly understood by every one concerned in it when I say that certain indirect charges now levied upon steam-ships are much more likely to diminish this trade than either the comparatively trivial port and landing charges made by the Government on vessels entering the harbour, or the duty that should be imposed on the consignees or agents of such vessels of helping instead of retarding the action of the Customs Department.

Advantages of the Proposed Changes.

106. By the adoption of the improvements I have suggested, a considerable economy of labour would be effected, the despatch of business would be promoted, and the Customs revenue would be increased, without entailing anything unreasonable upon the trade. As in most eastern countries, it is too much the habit for the Government to perform services for the people which the people ought to be left to do for themselves. This habit, together with the lack of energy resulting from the climate and from the temperament of the native population, appears to me to account in a great measure for whatever numerical excess is to be found in the Civil Service of Malta.

The Efficient Management of the Department.

107. While pointing out the defects that I have observed in the working of the Customs Department, it is due to the gentleman who presides over it that I should here testify to the energy and talent with which, making good use of all the powers assigned to him, he has effected many important reforms in its administration, and thus rendered

efficient service to the Government, with the approval of all classes of the community. That approval found expression in the annual address of the President of the Chamber of Commerce to the Members of the Exchange in 1876, when he said, "The Chamber of Commerce cannot abstain from proffering a word of praise to the present Collector of Customs, the Hon. F. V. Inglott, for the many improvements introduced by him in the internal organisation of the Department, all yielding results more than satisfactory as regards the general interests of the trade." The Customs Department.

108. The Chamber of Commerce has asked for the appointment of a second Assistant Gauger, in order to prevent vexatious delays in passing imported liquids into consumption. As this request is endorsed by the Collector, who has convinced me that the revenue may be expected to benefit to an extent that will more than cover the expense, I recommend that it be acceded to. Proposed Changes in the Establishment.

109. It is not easy to estimate the exact saving of time and labour that will result from the various changes that I have proposed; but, especially if use be made of the copying-press, I believe that they will justify the reduction of at least one, if not two, in the number of Clerks, besides enabling those who remain to do their work more thoroughly.

THE PORT DEPARTMENT.

110. The duties usually performed by a Harbour Master are in Malta assigned to the Superintendent of Ports, who is so styled in order to distinguish him from the Harbour Master attached to Her Majesty's Dockyards. As he is in frequent communication with the naval authorities and with the commanders of the Queen's ships, it is considered necessary that he should be himself an officer who has served in the Royal Navy. He has control over the entrances to all the harbours of Malta and Gozo, and is responsible for the maintenance of discipline and good order in them as regards pilotage, the mooring of ships, the superintendence of lighthouses and the like. He is also *ex officio* member of the Board of Health, and Chief Quarantine Officer, as well as Shipping Master under the Merchant Shipping Act of 1854. Receiving a salary of £300 a year, his indoor establishment comprises an Assistant Superintendent at £150, and four Clerks and two Messengers, who receive in all £471 a year. The outdoor establishment consists of thirteen Keepers of Lighthouses and other buildings, and of twenty-six Boatmen, receiving in all £824 a year, to which are added in the Annual Estimates, sums of £87 for the hire of extra boats, boatmen and labourers, and of £133 for allowances and contingencies. The fees collected under the Merchant Shipping Act, varying from about £150 to nearly £300 a year, are divided, in proportions of two-thirds and one-third, between the Superintendent and the Assistant Superintendent of Ports. The Port Department. The Superintendent of Ports and his Staff.

111. The most important functions of the Port Department are executed in a very anomalous way. All ships entering either of the Valletta harbours are boarded by the Marine Police. This branch of the service was formerly under the control of the Superintendent of Quarantine and Marine Police, whose duty it was not only to see that all vessels were duly disposed of in the harbours and that Port dues were collected, but also either to give them *pratique* or to place them under quarantine, as well as to protect the revenue accruing to the Customs Department. This arrangement appears to have worked well, but as to the Marine Police was also entrusted the general maintenance of order within the harbours, and on the waterside, they were afterwards associated with the Interior Police under the management of the Superintendent of that body, without, however, their duties as revenue and quarantine agents being taken from them. For some time past, accordingly, the Adjutant of Marine Police has had his headquarters in the same building as the Customs and the Port Departments, and has co-operated with the heads of those establishments in performing the services required by them without their exercising any formal authority over him. The members of that force thus act as regular policemen under the Superintendent of Police, and by courtesy both as boarding and *pratique* agents under the Superintendent of Ports and as revenue protectors and landing-waiters under the Collector of Customs. Anomalous Arrangements for Boarding Ships. The Marine Police.

112. It may be economical and convenient that they should continue to be charged with all these various duties, as otherwise the number of men employed about the harbours would have to be greatly increased; but I believe that the duties would be much more satisfactorily conducted if the Marine Police establishment were placed under the direct control of the Superintendent of Ports, that officer being held responsible for the due performance of the services of that body in connection with the Customs and the Police Departments. The strictly police duties of the Marine Police are at present Proposed Transfer of the Marine Police to the Port Department.

The Port Department.	of less importance than the others, and it is to be expected that they will be efficiently performed under the direction of a competent Adjutant, responsible to the Superintendent of Ports, and, if the change which I propose be made, there ought to be no difficulty in converting the men into a far more useful body of revenue protectors than they now appear to be. The subordinating of more to less important functions has necessarily caused the principal services with which they are entrusted to be made of less account than they should be.
	113. In such a port as Valletta, which steamers are allowed to enter and to quit within a few hours, performing all their operations, if it suits them, during the night, it is of extreme importance that all the agents of the Harbour Master should be energetic, intelligent, and honest men. To secure such men it might even be expedient to pay them at a higher rate than is now allowed, though that is higher than the scale of pay appointed for the Interior Police. It is absolutely necessary, at any rate, that they should be superior men, and that, having to be in constant communication with Englishmen and with foreigners who are more likely to be acquainted with English than with Maltese or even Italian, they should all have a satisfactory knowledge of the English language.
The Coast-guards.	114. About eighty members of the Interior Police Force, stationed along the coasts of Malta and Gozo, are partly, if not mainly, employed in performing coastguard duties. If it is not found convenient to place them entirely under the control of the Superintendent of Ports, his authority over them, in so far as they act as guardians of the revenue, ought to be much more clearly defined than at present.
Quarantine Duties.	115. By the return to the old order of things as regards the Marine Police, which I propose, the quarantine duties of the Port Department might be more efficiently performed than they now are. To render these duties as serviceable as they should be, it is necessary that every incoming ship should be met before she enters port by the *pratique* officer, who in Malta is a member of the Marine Police Force, and, unless a clean bill of health can be shown, at once sent into quarantine. Through the absence of direct control by the Superintendent of Ports, and in consequence of the prevalent notion in Malta that it is allowable to run great risks in order to facilitate as much as possible the rapid passage of steamships through the port, the business of the *pratique* agent appears often to be done in a most perfunctory manner.
Proposed Charge for Bills of Health.	116. Great care, on the other hand, is taken in granting bills of health to outgoing ships. Contrary to the usage of other ports, no charge is made for this service, which entails considerable work on the Department, as, upon an average, five or six sailing-vessels and from six to ten steamers quit the Port every day. I endorse Mr. Rowsell's recommendation that a charge of five shillings be made in the case of ships of more than 100 tons' burthen, and a charge of two shillings and sixpence for all smaller vessels. This would secure to the revenue an addition of at least £700 or £800 a year.
Proposed Fees on Pilots' Licences.	117. There are at present about fifty pilots employed in and about the harbours of Malta, all of whom are examined and licensed by the Superintendent of Ports, but who pay no fees either for examination or for licence. I am of opinion that a charge of ten shillings should be made for the first licence, and that this should be renewed annually, on condition of good conduct, on payment of five shillings.
Proposed Charges on Licences for Pontoons and Cargo Boats.	118. In the harbours there are also about three hundred pontoons or lighters, and fifty cargo or ballast boats. The pontoons almost monopolize the inner dock or basin in the Grand Harbour near the Marsa, and take up much room in the Pietà branch of the Quarantine Harbour. Enjoying all the benefits of the port, not as ordinary vessels coming and going, but as floating coal-depôts which encumber it perpetually, they contribute nothing whatever towards its maintenance, though their owners or employers are generally admitted to be among the most prosperous traders in Valletta. I consider that their proprietors should be required to obtain licences for them, on payment of ten shillings a year. In the same manner I propose that five shillings a year should be charged for licences to cargo or ballast boats.
Proposed Charges on Licences to Boats and Boatmen.	119. I am of opinion, moreover, that a small charge should be made for licences to the numerous boats and boatmen employed in conveying passengers about the harbours. An annual fee of two shillings and sixpence for each boat, and of one shilling for each boatman, would not press heavily on them, and would at the same time help to maintain discipline.
Floating Tanks.	120. Several floating tanks, which obtain water from the public fountains in order to supply it to ships visiting the port, should either be licensed and required to pay an annual fee, or be charged for the water.
Steam-tugs.	121. Steam-tugs should also be charged an annual fee of reasonable amount for permission to make use of the harbours.
Collection of Fees.	122. It would simplify and ensure the collection of all fees for licences in connection

with the Port Department, if they were issued by the Customs Department on the authority of certificates from the Superintendent of Ports. ^{THE PORT DEPARTMENT.}

123. A number of men, with the sanction of the Superintendent of Ports but not under his control, are now employed, and paid by the masters, to act as guardians of vessels calling at the port. This arrangement does not appear to work well, and I endorse the suggestion of the Assistant Superintendent that a corps of about 30 authorised guardians, or so many as may be found necessary, be established, wearing a badge or uniform, and receiving the ordinary labourers' or boatmen's wages of £30 a year, but without any claim to superannuation, and that a charge of four shillings for every day or part of a day be made by the Government upon each ship requiring their services. ^{Guardians of Vessels.}

124. For the salaries of the Keepers and Assistant Keepers of the Lighthouses and Towers at St. Elmo, Fort Ricasoli, Fort Tigne, Delimara, and Gozo, an annual expense of £242 is incurred, and the estimated charge for oil and other necessaries is £440. Some of the custodians are unable to read or write, and this necessarily aggravates the laxity with which the store accounts are kept. Supplies are obtained by the Keepers from the contractors whenever they are required, and the only control on the consumption is a very partial and irregular inspection. No men should be employed who cannot keep simple accounts, and these accounts should be checked by periodical surveys. I am of opinion that the lamps should be adapted to the use of, and supplied with, petroleum instead of olive oil. Not only would the lights thereby gain in brilliancy and cost much less, but, as petroleum is not fit for cooking and other domestic purposes to which oil can be applied, the risk of misappropriation would be greatly reduced. ^{Lighthouses and their Keepers.}

125. I have nothing to say as to the way in which the duties of Shipping Master under the Merchant Shipping Act are performed by the Superintendent and the Assistant Superintendent of Ports, except that it appears to me to be very satisfactory. The system of remuneration by division of fees, however, is objectionable, and should not, in my opinion, be continued in the case of the successors to the present occupants of the office. ^{Shipping Master's Duties.}

126. The slight duties now performed in the Chief Secretary's office on behalf of the Governor, who is *ex officio* Registrar under the Merchant Shipping Act, may with advantage be transferred to the Port Department.* ^{Registrar's Duties under the Merchant Shipping Act.}

127. Considering that the proposed reunion of the Marine Police with the Port Department, and the other changes I have suggested, will throw additional clerical work on the office, I do not propose any reduction of its staff. By using a small copying-press and removing some redundancies in the registers and account-books, however, I believe that sufficient economy of time and labour may be effected to provide for the new duties assigned to it. ^{* See par. 80.}

POLICE AND PRISONS.

128. The charges in the Estimates for 1879 on account of the Police Establishments of Malta and Gozo, including both Interior and Marine Police and what are known as the Medical Police, as well as the small prisons and lock-ups in Valletta and Gozo, amount to £20,416 5s. 3d. Further charges, amounting to £3694, are made on account of the Corradino Prison; and the expenses of the small Prison for Women at Floriana are mixed up with the accounts of the Charitable Institutions. ^{POLICE AND PRISONS.}

129. The Interior Police Force, which performs coast-guard duties as well as being responsible for the maintenance of order in the cities and country districts, though not in the harbours of Valletta, consists of an Adjutant, receiving £280 a year and £35 for transport, thirteen Inspectors and Sub-Inspectors, whose salaries range from £120 to £60 a year, six Sergeant-majors at £45, fourteen Sergeants at £40, and three hundred and six Constables, receiving £35, £30, or £27, according to their class. ^{The Interior Police Force.}

130. I cannot pretend to offer any opinion as to the numerical sufficiency of this force, but I hear on all sides complaints as to its quality. It appears that, though the pay is fully up to the average of the wages of the class from which enlistments are made, the service is so repugnant to the feelings of the population that applicants for admission into it are often of very questionable character, and it is considered necessary to accept them without sufficient evidence of previous good conduct; that they are not enlisted for any fixed period, and can relinquish their employment at a day's notice; and that they undergo no sort of preparatory training, and are subjected, after appointment, to very little discipline. Two-thirds of them are unable to write their names, a much larger proportion are ignorant of the English language, and many speak nothing but ^{Its Unsatisfactory Condition.}

POLICE AND PRISONS.

Suggestions for improving it.

Maltese. No periodical reports seem to be made by the Superintendent as to the organisation, efficiency, and character of the force, but its condition is evidently by no means such as should be expected in a body of men intended to protect the public against evil-doers.

131. It is possible that the work would be more effectively done by a smaller body of trained men drawn from a more respectable portion of the community. If no reduction of numbers is thought expedient, however, it should be considered whether some additional expense would not be wisely incurred in improving the tone and character of the force by subjecting the men to proper discipline, and especially by teaching them the rudiments of a policeman's duty before placing them on active service in the streets. It should be made a condition of promotion to the first class of Constables, and yet more to the higher ranks, that every man so promoted should be able to make himself understood in English, and a decided preference should be given to the same qualification in recruits.

132. Adjutants, Inspectors, and Sub-Inspectors are at present drawn from the ranks. If the status of the corps could be so elevated as to attract young men from a different class of society, who might be able to pass moderate educational tests, the change in the whole body would doubtless be very beneficial.

The Superintendent of Police.

133. It is yet more important that a suitable occupant should be found for the office of Superintendent. The system hitherto adopted of assigning it to one or other of the Chief Clerks in the Civil Service, merely with the object of giving promotion, is, I consider, a faulty one, and largely responsible for the present unsatisfactory state of the force. The duties of a Superintendent of Police are such that, without special training, he can hardly be expected to interest himself in the work entrusted to him, or to be able to secure the assistance of his subordinates in performing it.

Systematic Inspections.

134. He or his deputies should pay frequent visits to all the stations under his management, both in Valletta, in the adjoining cities, and in the country districts, including those looked after by the Coast-guards, and at each station an inspection-book should be kept in which they should record the dates of their visits, and state the condition in which they found the staff there quartered. Such visits, when paid at all, appear now only to be paid in a most perfunctory way. In lieu of the fixed money allowances to cover travelling expenses made to the Superintendent, to the Adjutant of Interior Police, and to one of the Inspectors, the actual horse or carriage hire incurred by these officers during their visits of inspection should be charged in the public accounts.

The Marine Police Force.

135. The Marine Police Force comprises an Adjutant, receiving £150 a year, eight Inspectors and Sub-Inspectors, whose salaries range from £120 to £55, eight Sergeants at £45, ninety-seven Constables at £38 and £32, and two Searchers at £90 and £60. This corps, being somewhat better paid, appears to be less faulty than the Interior Police Force. It is capable of improvement, however, and this, I hope, may be secured by its transference to the Port Department, as I have already proposed.* That change need not interfere with the existing plan of promoting suitable men from the Interior to the Marine Police.

* See par. 112.

The Medical Police.

136. For the establishment of Medical Police, as it is called, a sum of £1459 is charged in the estimates under the head of Police. As the Superintendent has nothing to do with the control of this establishment, I propose that he be relieved of its nominal custody, and that it be included among the Charitable Institutions.†

† See par. 176.

Proposed Reductions in the Police Department.

137. By thus limiting the responsibilities of the Superintendent of Police to the duties that properly devolve upon such an officer, his work will be considerably reduced, and I am of opinion that, when a vacancy occurs, the salary attached to the post may, without injury to the public service, be altered from £500 to £400 a year. By relieving his office, moreover, of the clerical duties connected with the Marine and Medical Police, and by adopting other improvements which I have already in part foreshadowed, I consider that two of the four Clerks now under him may be removed to other branches of the service, so as to eliminate from the Department everything that has no affinity with its proper functions.

Contracts for Police Services.

138. All contracts now made by the Superintendent of Police, including those for the supply of forage and oil, and the sweeping and watering of streets, should be entered into by the Director of Contracts on information furnished by the Police authorities.‡

‡ See par. 87.

Civil Status Returns.

139. As it is prescribed by law that all returns of births, deaths, and marriages should be recorded in the Public Registry, the repetition of them in the Police Office appears to be quite unnecessary.§

§ See par. 209.

Mortality Returns.

140. The compilation of the fortnightly and annual mortality returns now made in the Police Office in order to be published by the Chief Police Physician should, as far as it is held desirable to continue them in their present elaborate form, be transferred to the Sanitary Office.‖

‖ See par. 184.

141. The issuing of licences for the sale of wines and spirits, for billiard-tables, for shooting, for opening shops, for using carriages and carts, for hawkers, for permission to alter or construct buildings, and all others now prepared by the Police, should be transferred to the Receiver-General's Department,* with the exception of boat and boatmen's licences, which, as I have already recommended, should be issued from the Customs Department.† In the case of all licences with which the Police authorities are concerned, they should only be expected to furnish certificates of character for the satisfaction of the Licensing Departments. Such of these licences as are now issued free, numbering in all three or four thousand, should be charged for at reasonable rates, if not as a source of revenue, at any rate to an extent that would cover the cost of issue. POLICE AND PRISONS.
Licences.
* See par. 66.
† See par. 122.

142. Of the licences now granted by the Superintendent of Police, by far the most important are those for the sale of wines and spirits. Prior to 1873 an annual charge of £2 was made for every licence applying to Valletta, Floriana, and the "Three Cities" of Cospicua, Senglea, and Vittoriosa, and of 5s. for all the "country" districts, including even the important suburb of Sliema. During several years before that time, the efforts of some philanthropists in Malta had prevented the indiscriminate issue of new licences, and the number of licensed houses had been kept within nearly the same limits. In 1872-3 the number of £2 licences in force was 527, and that of 5s. licences was 529 for the "country" districts of Malta, and 128 for Gozo. In 1873, however, partly with a view to increase the revenue, partly to meet the complaints of persons who were debarred by the existing rule from opening "grog-shops," as they are generally styled, the charge for city licences was raised from £2 to £4, that for country licences remaining at 5s., and they were issued almost indiscriminately, the only limit being that the Police authorities were expected not to grant them to notoriously bad characters. Immediately after this change of law and policy, a vast number of new licences were applied for and obtained, and, though some of the speculations then entered into soon failed, the permanent increase in the number of "grog-shops" has been very considerable. In 1877-8 there were issued 570 licences at £4, and 973 for Malta and 138 for Gozo at 5s. Wine and Spirit Licences.
The "Grog-shops" of Malta.

143. It hardly falls within my province to recommend either that, with a view to increasing the revenue, the charge for licences should be increased, or that, in the interests of morality, the number of "grog-shops" should be limited; but the subject is so important, and excites so much alarm and distress among all residents in Malta who have the well-being of the people at heart, that I may be excused for briefly referring to it. In Valletta there is now a "grog-shop" for every seventy-five of its inhabitants, including women and children. In addition to these there are of course the soldiers and sailors, who are the principal frequenters of many of these establishments; but as regards the former the canteen arrangements of the military authorities suffice for all their requirements, and nothing but needless temptation is thrown in their way by the low houses which face them whenever they pass in or out of their barracks. The misfortune is not only that an altogether unnecessary number of "grog-shops" are to be found in Malta, ranging side by side in frequent rows of three or four in some of the thoroughfares, but the great competition thus provoked leads on the one hand to the adulteration of beer, wine and spirits, often, it is said, with poisonous ingredients, and on the other to the barefaced exhibition of such allurements as may come from the presence of women, whose costumes, words and gestures can leave no passer-by in doubt as to their character. It is evident that no sort of effective surveillance is exercised over these "grog-shops," and that in renewing licences the authorities put a very liberal interpretation indeed upon the rule that the granting of them is conditional upon good behaviour. Seeing what a numerous staff of Sanitary Officers is in the pay of the Government, moreover, it is strange that little or nothing is done to test the liquors sold in the licensed houses, in order—if scientific confirmation is given to the popular impression that they are largely adulterated by cheap and unwholesome stimulants and narcotics—to prevent such dishonest practices.

144. Of the wine and spirit licences issued outside of Valletta and the "Three Cities," a large number appear to be taken out by grocers and general store-dealers, who supply their customers with only a few bottles of cheap wine in the course of a year, on whom 5s. is a tax quite heavy enough to impose for the useful service they render to the community. In the principal villages and towns, however, and especially in such a prosperous suburb of the capital as Sliema, a much larger and very different trade is carried on; and to charge there only 5s. for a privilege which within the cities themselves is valued at £4, is certainly unreasonable.

145. Without wishing to do more than call attention to these matters, I may say that it appears to me very desirable that, whatever other limits may be fixed as regards the issuing of wine and spirit licences, care should be taken to withhold them from

Police and Prisons.	applicants of bad character who are known to sell adulterated and unwholesome liquors and to allow vicious persons to assemble in their houses; and I would also suggest that, in any revision of the present charges for licences, suitable distinctions should be made between small tradespeople both in town and in the country, more extensive dealers in the cheap wines which are ordinarily consumed by the Maltese, and the proprietors of what are known throughout Malta as "grog-shops."
Corradino Prison.	146. I need say very little about the Corradino Prison, which appears to be very successfully managed by its present Superintendent, who, however, complains that the
The Correctional Wards.	arrangements of the correctional wards render it impossible to maintain among the prisoners such strict discipline as is desirable, and that the state of the law as regards
The Reformatory.	juvenile offenders, which causes them to be punished as ordinary prisoners during short periods, instead of being subjected to longer and more humane reformatory treatment, renders useless the well-conceived appliances for industrial training which have lately been added to the establishment.
The Prison Inspector.	147. As fortnightly visits of inspection are made to the prison by Commissioners appointed by the Governor, the office of Inspector, now held by the Senior Police Magistrate with allowances amounting to £70 a year, seems to be almost a sinecure, and it may, I think, be abolished on the retirement of the present occupant.
The Warders and Assistant Superintendent.	148. Out of the saving thus effected, it might be well to augment by £2 or £3 the scanty allowance of £4 a year each now made to the Assistant Chief Warder and nine Warders in lieu of quarters, and perhaps also to make some addition to the £10 allowed to the Assistant Superintendent for house-rent.
The Catholic and Protestant Chaplains.	149. The Roman Catholic inmates of the prison have the services both of a Chaplain and of an Assistant Chaplain. As there are always several Englishmen in the establishment whose cost is in many. cases defrayed from Imperial sources, it would be reasonable to make some provision for the expenses incurred by the Protestant Chaplain to the Government in his ministrations to them.
Contracts.	150. Contracts for the provisions supplied for the prisoners' diet should form part of the general contracts for articles of food, which, as I have proposed, should be made by
* See par. 87.	the Director of Contracts.*

THE CHARITABLE INSTITUTIONS.

The Charitable Institutions.	151. Sums amounting to £26,883, or rather more than one-sixth of the entire expenditure of the Local Government, are charged in the Annual Estimates on account of the various Charitable Institutions maintained in Malta and Gozo, including the amount annually voted for out-door relief. In that total no account is taken of the value of the buildings thus occupied, some of which have been erected in recent times at considerable expense; of the cost of repairs and additions to these several buildings, which is heavy and constant; of the pensions granted to the numerous employés retired from the institutions, and from the Controller's Department; of the pay, allowances and pensions of the large establishment of Medical Police, who are little more than agents for the dispensing of charity; of the machinery for almost entirely gratuitous education throughout the Islands; or of the very questionable favour shown in encouraging and promoting litigation. Even without taking account of the last two items, if the other charges be included in the general amount, the expenditure in "charity" will be found to exceed one-fifth of the whole revenue of the Colony.
The old Foundations.	152. An erroneous impression prevails that the duty of maintaining all these establishments is imposed on the Government by the terms on which it succeeded to the property held by the Knights of the Order of St. John. That property certainly
† See Appendix B.(II.).	includes certain foundations intended to be applied in charitable ways.† Thus the Hospital of Santo Spirito was formerly administered out of the proceeds of several endowments, which now yield in rentals about £460 a year. The Magdalen Asylum, moreover, claims to be supported at public expense because the Government now derives nearly £600 a year from property originally possessed by a convent founded for the reception of penitent women. In like manner the Hospital for Incurables, open to both sexes, may be regarded as entitled to all the proceeds of the "Fondazione Scappi," begun in 1626, and subsequently augmented with the object of keeping up an asylum for poor women suffering from incurable complaints. There are also some other foundations, now managed by the Land Revenue Department, portions of which were intended to be used in charitable ways. The "Fondazione Assemblea," for instance, among other objects provided for alms to be distributed amongst the poor, and for marriage portions to two

poor girls every year; while of the "Cumulo di Carità," composed of various bequests now yielding about £540 a year, a part was to be applied in providing marriage portions, part in buying wheat to be distributed generally among the poor, and part in giving alms to the needy in special districts. It would be difficult, if not impossible, to ascertain the exact present value of all these charitable bequests, apart from the other objects of the old foundations; but I believe that the total, if it could be arrived at, would come very far short of £3000 a year—that is, would not supply the amount now spent in out-door relief, to say nothing of the hospitals, asylums, and other institutions, which cost nearly ten times as much. Whatever justification, therefore, is to be found for the elaborate system of so-called charity, which regards every working-man, however lucrative his employment, and his belongings, as fit objects for charity, it must not be looked for in any supposed moral or equitable obligation devolving on the present Government to maintain the institutions of the Knights of St. John. The Charitable Institutions.

153. It is beyond my province, however, to call in question the policy that governs the treatment of the poor in these Islands; nor shall I venture to offer any remarks on what has been represented to me as want of discrimination in selecting the fittest objects for admission to, and for relief by, the several establishments. The machinery for determining such questions—comprising a Controller of Charitable Institutions and his staff of five Clerks, aided by six unpaid Commissioners of Charity, and a very large number of professional and non-professional employés—is elaborate enough for the attainment of the end in view; but all organisations of this nature depend so largely on those who have to work them, that I am afraid any general criticisms I could make would be of little value, and I shall, therefore, only throw out a few suggestions, and call attention to the more prominent matters in which improvements appear to me to be especially needed. The present Establishments.

154. Nine separate or associated establishments in Malta, and two in Gozo, are included in the system of Charitable Institutions for which the Controller has to provide. The Central Civil Hospital.

155. The most important, and one of the most useful, is the Central Civil Hospital at Floriana, in which the daily average of patients is one hundred and seventy. Both its site and its structure are, on many grounds, objectionable. It is placed over barracks occupied by a regiment of soldiers, to whom it offers a dangerous focus of disease at a distance of only a few yards from their dormitories and day-rooms, while at the same time the patients suffer from the clamour of military activity. I am told that cases of concussion of the brain, more particularly, have been known to be much aggravated by the noise of bugles and drums which is inevitable. The building, moreover, originally projected and occupied as an Orphanage for Female Children, is ill-adapted for a hospital. The ventilation of many of its wards appears to be very defective, and, when all the beds are occupied, especially during an epidemic, the spread of infection can hardly be avoided. These are defects inherent to the present building, and there are others that can only be removed at considerable expense. The drainage is on the old system of wide and deep sewers of rock or stone, the porous character of which causes the retention of odours which glazed pipes would prevent. The water supply is insufficient, and the arrangements for hot-water circulation, obtained from a separate fire instead of from the kitchen, are cumbersome and costly. The kitchen itself, besides being very small and poorly lighted, is situated underground at one end of the building, so as to render impossible the prompt distribution of the food prepared in it. The wash-house is also small and badly placed, and might with great advantage be removed to the side of a neighbouring ditch, by means of which the dirty water could be got rid of and the risk of infection lessened. Almost more objectionable is the contiguity of the dead-house to one of the wards, especially as it is also used as a post-mortem examination room, in which are deposited not only the bodies of persons who have died on the premises, but also others brought from the town and the waterside, sometimes in a most obnoxious condition. Its Structural Defects.

156. The professional staff of the hospital, comprising, besides two Visiting Physicians and Surgeons, three resident professional men, appears to me unnecessarily large. Were the latter precluded from private practice, it might be well, when a vacancy occurs, to divide between two the salaries now paid to three, in order to secure the constant attendance of skilled practitioners. The employment of two apothecaries and medical store-keepers may perhaps be necessary, but if so, they should both be well-instructed and energetic persons, able to maintain a better system than at present prevails. The depôt in which medicines are stored, and from which they are supplied to all the other dispensaries in the Island, should be arranged with more regard to order and to the preservation of its contents. And as regards the distribution of medicines to patients on the establishment, much benefit might result from one of the Sisters of Charity being Its Professional Staff.

THE CHARIT-
ABLE INSTITU-
TIONS.

Sisters of
Charity and
Nurses.

English
Patients.

Religious
Attendance.

The Hospital
of Santo
Spirito.

The Hospital
for Incur-
ables.

charged with the duty of administering them at the prescribed times, under the doctor's orders.

157. The recent employment of Sisters of Charity as matrons and superintendents of nurses and female servants, both here and elsewhere, appears to be an admirable innovation. These ladies, however, by their religious vows and the conditions on which they enter the public service, are precluded from certain occupations in the hospital for which intelligence and good discipline are essential, and which are very unsatisfactorily performed by their native assistants. The structural defects of the kitchen and wash-house are not solely to blame for the unsatisfactory condition in which I found them on the occasion of my visit, and there is room for yet more improvement as regards the nurses employed in the wards. Married women, admitted without proper training, too much occupied to acquire useful experience while in the service, and nearly always with infants of their own to look after and nourish, cannot be expected to attend satisfactorily to the patients entrusted to their care. If it is not possible to obtain really competent persons for this duty, the nurses ought at any rate to be selected from those who are not constantly subjected to the pressing claims of maternity. They ought also to receive their meals on the premises instead of going out for them, and to have a change of raiment, so as to be able to maintain a greater show of cleanliness and decency.

158. The depressing influences of the hospital appear to weigh most heavily on the English and English-speaking patients, generally sailors, who have a special claim to consideration, seeing that, unlike most of the others, their maintenance is paid for at the rate of 1s. 6d. a day. A separate ward, for which space would be available if the number of Resident Medical Officers were reduced from three to two, should be provided for them, attended by two English nurses, who could reply intelligently to their inquiries and meet their reasonable wants. Their food, too, though slightly different from that of the natives, is not what it ought to be.

159. Considering the facility with which temporary assistance can be obtained from the immediate neighbourhood of the establishment, the employment of two resident Roman Catholic Chaplains in it hardly seems to be necessary. On the other hand, it would be only reasonable that some provision should be made for the expenses incurred by the English Chaplain to the Government in his ministrations to the Protestant patients.

160. Whatever reforms may be required in the Central Civil Hospital, there appears to be much greater need of change in the management of the Hospital of Santo Spirito, in the outskirts of Città Vecchia. Though an old building, erected more than four hundred years ago, and faulty in some respects, its extreme unpopularity with the natives can scarcely be due to any structural defects. No one who enters it, however, can fail to be impressed by the gloominess of its appearance, which must be attributed to the evident want of energy in turning it to good account as a curative establishment. Its resident doctor is charged with duties as a Police Physician elsewhere, and its Superintendent who is also its Visiting Physician is in the same position, while both are at liberty to eke out their scanty incomes, if possible, by private practice. It now receives an average of forty-five patients of all sorts. I am of opinion that it could be put to much better use than at present by being converted into a Convalescent Hospital in connection with the Central Hospital, which in that case would have more room for patients suffering from serious illnesses. If a small ward were retained for the reception of urgent cases brought from the neighbourhood, or from the parts of the Island more remote from Floriana, the rest might be available for patients in greater need of the healthy air in which it is situated than of much medical attendance. A single professional officer might then suffice for it, with benefit to the inmates and with a reduction of expense.

161. There would be great advantage, moreover, in removing the Hospital for Incurables, if possible, from its present locality. Lodged in the lower part of Valletta, near to Fort St. Elmo, in an incommodious building formed of two old houses, its situation is unsuitable alike to its unfortunate inmates and to the inhabitants round about. It has no day-rooms or airing-grounds, the female patients are only allowed to take exercise on the roof, while the men furnish a painful spectacle when promenading on the neighbouring granaries. Very few improvements appear to be practicable so long as the institution remains where it now is; and, as soon as the Government can see its way to do so, it would be well to transfer it to Città Vecchia or some other place where it would be near enough to another establishment for a safe economy in medical supervision to be effected. When the long-promised new spizio is built, the most convenient arrangement might be to make the structure large enough to include an asylum for the two hundred and twenty or more victims of incurable disease whom the Government undertakes to provide for, and whose chief requirements are wholesome food, provisions for cleanliness, and fresh air. It may be observed that the building

at Città Vecchia, on which the Government spent about £600 some time ago in adapting it to such a purpose, and which is in every way well fitted for it, does not appear to be now made much use of by the military authorities to whom it was handed over to be occupied as a sanitarium.

THE CHARITABLE INSTITUTIONS.

162. The Lunatic Asylum near to Città Vecchia, containing about four hundred inmates, is the only one of the more modern buildings in Malta that was erected for the purpose to which it is applied. The site chosen for it, however, was most unsuitable, and it was copied from a bad model. In the way of organisation much appears to have been done towards neutralising the bad influence of its original construction; but it strikes me that some further alterations may be effected by a Superintendent well acquainted with hygienic laws and familiar with the most approved methods of dealing with mental disease. A Turkish bath might be erected with advantage, and, if the water-supply were improved, more use of it could be made in the establishment without exacting from the male patients so much labour in pumping. There is a notable lack of healthy occupation and diversion for the inmates, partly due to the fact that the asylum is built on a barren rock, but not sufficiently atoned for by internal arrangements. The professional staff of the asylum—two Resident Medical Officers being directed by a Visiting Physician who is nominally aided by two other professional members of the Medical Board—appears to be certainly large enough, but it might be advantageously strengthened, if possible, by the addition to the Board of an experienced Army Medical Officer. As the relatives of inmates, if they can afford to pay for or contribute to their maintenance, are required to do so, careful periodical inquiries on this subject ought to be made. I am assured on good authority that such inquiries at the present time would considerably reduce the cost of maintenance.

The Lunatic Asylum.

163. The establishment most in need of reform, however, is the Ospizio, or Asylum for the Aged and Infirm Poor, with an average population of nearly seven hundred persons, and with three smaller institutions connected or combined with it—the Female Prison, in which on an average nineteen persons are detained and subjected to mild forms of punishment; the Magdalen Asylum, containing about fifteen voluntary inmates; and the Foundling Hospital, in which last year sixteen young children were being nursed.

The Ospizio.

164. This building, situated in the lowest levels of the fortifications of Floriana, was originally constructed to serve as a powder-mill for the Government of the Knights of St. John. For that purpose it may have been well adapted, but it is altogether unsuitable to its present object. Though in several parts numerous alterations and improvements appear to have been made from time to time, its original form and distribution still remain, and throw insuperable difficulties in the way of proper organisation and discipline. The building is, in fact, a huge labyrinth, which offers very great facilities for the commission of all sorts of irregularities, to which the curious aggregation of institutions within it necessarily conduces. The only effective improvement that can be made is to separate from it some, if not all, of these minor institutions, and to construct with as little delay as possible the new Poor House long since promised by the Government, though postponed in deference to what were supposed to be the stronger claims for a new Opera House.

165. The new Ospizio should be made to accommodate none but the aged poor of both sexes having no friends or kindred to assist them. Many inmates of the Hospital for Incurables might, however, be properly included in that category. So long as it is considered necessary in Malta to maintain all old persons who have failed to make provision for themselves and who have no other means of support, the work ought to be done satisfactorily, though without lavish expenditure or such adjuncts as would tend to demoralise the poor by encouraging them to be improvident. The Ospizio, not being a curative institution, should not be made in any way attractive.

166. While it seems to be necessary to wait for the new building to be constructed before any considerable improvements can be hoped for, and while it does not devolve upon me to attempt any general scheme for those improvements, I think that immediate benefit would result from a reform of the dietary of the Ospizio. The three meals a day prescribed by regulations should be given, instead of only two as at present, and by the introduction of a greater variety of vegetable food some economy might be effected without any prejudice to the inmates.

167. As crime appears to be rare amongst the women of Malta, and, when committed, to be best dealt with by very light punishment, it may be desirable that the small Female Prison should continue to be classed among the Charitable Institutions, and left under the amiable custody of a Sister of Charity. If, when the new Ospizio is built, the prison is planted in the immediate neighbourhood of that establishment or of the Hospital for Incurables, the wash-house of one or both can furnish an economical and convenient

The Prison for Women.

THE CHARITABLE INSTITUTIONS.opportunity for the performance of such hard labour as the prisoners are condemned to.

The Magdalen Asylum.168. I see no advantage in continuing the Magdalen Asylum. There are private religious establishments in the Island in which the young women to whom it now offers a temporary residence without charge are likely to be better looked after than can be expected in a Government institution. Instead of maintaining it, it would be better, if it were still deemed necessary to spend any money on such an object, to subsidise one of those establishments. I do not, however, recommend this course, as I consider that the Government already does far more for the people in the way of so-called charity than is really beneficial to them.

The Foundling Hospital.169. Without waiting for any other change in the Ospizio, I think that the Foundling Hospital should be removed to the same premises as the Orphan Asylum and amalgamated with it. So much space would thus be saved in the Ospizio that the estimated expense of £150 in increasing the Female Prison, which is now proposed, need not be incurred. The Sisters of Charity in charge of the Orphan Asylum, and perhaps some of the elder girls therein, might be expected to take much better care of the infants, after they are weaned, than their present native nurses.

The Orphan Asylum.170. At the same time the Orphan Asylum, which accommodates about one hundred and twenty-five children, may be considerably improved. Situated in the lower part of Valletta, near to the Hospital for Incurables, the building, which was originally a Magdalen Asylum, is very defective in form, distribution, and accommodation. There being no grounds or sufficient exercising-yards, no opportunities for physical education offer themselves, and the mental training is insufficient. I am informed that, when the children leave the school at the prescribed age, they know very little Italian and nothing at all of English. They should be fitted to make their way as servants, mechanics, and tradesmen, and it would be well if a small training-ship could without much expense be procured, in which some of the boys, as well as others outside the asylum, might learn to become sailors. As inconveniences are said to arise from the presence of both boys and girls in the same building, it would seem desirable, if it can be done, to transfer the girls, with the infants brought from the Foundling Hospital, to a house in the country, suitable for an industrial school, and to leave the whole building in town for the male division only. Orphans of one parent could, in that case, be more frequently admitted on payment, as is allowed by the regulations.

The Civil Hospital and the Ospizio at Gozo.171. Concerning the two charitable institutions at Gozo, the Civil Hospital and the Ospizio, I need say little. The hospital, which has room for a much larger number of patients than the average of twenty-one placed in it last year, is on the whole a suitable building for the purpose, though constructed a century and a half ago; and the adjoining Ospizio, which dates only from 1851, offers convenient accommodation to its one hundred and fifty-four inmates. The two establishments are united, as far as medical supervision goes, under the management of a visiting and a resident medical officer; and both are conducted on the same principles, and in obedience to the same regulations, as are in force at the larger kindred institutions in Malta.

Differences between Lay and Professional Authority.172. A difficulty common to all charitable organisations, and especially hospitals, lunatic asylums, and such establishments, is serious in this Colony. I refer to the confusion likely to arise from the division of authority between lay and professional directors. When the Charitable Institutions of Malta were reorganised and placed on their present footing, the Government was fortunate in commanding the services of an able medical man, who knew how, on occasion, to subordinate professional to lay interests, and who thus filled with great advantage the office of Inspector of Prisons and Charities to which he was appointed, and in which, according to the regulations then prepared, " being responsible to the Government for the good order, discipline, and economy of all these institutions," he was empowered "to inspect the performance of duty by every person belonging to them, whether officers or servants." It was not found desirable, however, to continue the office of Inspector after the death of Dr. Collins, and accordingly the office of Controller, formerly limited to the procuring of supplies for all Government establishments, has gained in importance without its lay occupant having as much authority over the professional staff or their relations with the other employés as the Inspector possessed. It appears to me very important that some such Proposed Appointment of an Army Medical Officer as Inspector or Visitor.authority should be exercised by a competent person, but I should not feel justified in recommending that it be vested in any professional man of Malta, nor can I hope that the Government will be able to appoint a lay Controller of Charitable Institutions, endowed with capacities for satisfactorily governing his professional as well as his lay subordinates. I therefore suggest that, if possible, arrangements should be made with the Imperial authorities for obtaining the assistance of an experienced army medical officer, who, in addition to being a member of the Lunatic Asylum Board, should act as inspector or visitor of all the medical establishments, with power to report to the Commissioners of Charity any defects or need for improvements observed by him in his occasional examinations of the hospitals, dispensaries and other establishments, and to whom reference could be made in case of any dispute between the Controller and the medical officers connected with his Department. I am convinced that any reasonable honorarium that might be accorded to such an officer would be an economical addition to the expenses of the Charitable Institutions. {The Charitable Institutions.}

173. If the Controller is thus at the same time relieved and assisted in his relations with the professional members of his staff, it will be easier for him to exercise an efficient control over its other branches. While being held responsible for the proper management of the clerical establishment in Valletta, and continuing to be an *ex officio* and the most responsible member of the Charity Commission, his principal duty should be to exercise constant supervision, by both periodical and surprisal visits, over each of the Charitable Institutions and all their sections and ramifications. The French system of having lay directors for professional institutions appears to me not only the best in itself, but also to be especially suitable to Malta. Competent medical men being appointed, no laymen should interfere with them in their professional duties, but those duties should be clearly defined, as they can be without difficulty, and the Controller should be master, as representative of the Government, in all questions involving principles of administration and discipline. The Superintendent of each institution, whether a professional man or a layman, should be responsible to him for all his non-professional duties, and it should be his business to see that those duties are satisfactorily performed. {Duties of the Controller.}

174. In making contracts for the supply of food, medicines, hospital stores, clothing, &c., and in providing for structural repairs and alterations, the Controller will be greatly assisted by the Director of Contracts who I propose should be appointed;* but it will be his duty to see that all such contracts and changes are properly fulfilled. He will also, of course, be responsible, as heretofore to the Treasury, henceforth the Receiver-General's Department, and to the Audit Office in all matters of account. {Contracts and Accounts. * See par. 87.}

175. The clerical duties of the Controller's establishment at Valletta appear to be satisfactorily performed. As the Controllership has been vacant during the period of my inquiry, and its duties have been executed by the Chief Clerk, with a consequent reduction in the strength of the staff, and as the Acting Controller informs me that the present Junior Clerk, on promotion, need not be replaced, I am justified in assuming that the nominal force of the Department is excessive. As, however, I shall presently propose that the clerical work connected with the Sanitary Board, now temporarily organised, be annexed, while it lasts, to the Department of Charitable Institutions,† and, as I have already proposed that certain duties now performed by a Clerk in the Police Department be transferred to that Board, I do not suggest any immediate reduction in the present authorised establishment of a Chief Clerk and four other Clerks, in addition to the Controller and the Deputy Controller in Gozo, who draws his salary as Deputy Collector of Land Revenue. The allowances to Clerk No. 1 of £10 "for services connected with the General Store," and £20 as Clerk to the Sanitary Board, should, however, be discontinued, and the Controller, instead of a fixed travelling allowance, should be provided with such transport as he requires. {The Controller's Staff. † See par. 181.}

176. I have already proposed that the body of professional men known as Medical Police now attached to the Superintendent of Police, but having no proper connection with his Department, and practically independent of all control by him, be considered henceforth as belonging to the Department of Charitable Institutions.‡ {The Medical Police. ‡ See par. 186.}

177. There are now twenty-five Police Physicians in Malta, and three in Gozo, besides the Chief Police Physician, who is supposed to be responsible for the performance of their duties. Those duties consist partly of attendance at fixed periods, generally twice or thrice every week, at the dispensaries attached to various police stations, of which there are forty-three in all, there to be consulted by and to prescribe for all poor persons in the several districts who may require medical or surgical assistance, and partly of such visiting of similar patients in their own houses at other times as may be necessary, serious cases being generally sent to one of the hospitals. Everybody in Malta who lives by daily labour, that is every working-man, as well as every beggar, is considered to have a claim to receive medical assistance and medicines gratuitously, when he or any member of his family is ill, and in consequence the large staff of Police Physicians has grown up in recent times. The salaries given, varying from £30 to £80 a year, though entitling them to pensions, are intended to be in effect only allowances, not precluding them from private practice. Only a few of them, however, appear to {Police Physicians.}

The Charitable Institutions.
have much other occupation. Many allege that the districts in which they live are too poor to contain paying patients, while others consider that the unpopularity brought upon them by the title of Police Physicians stands in the way of their being employed by any patients who can pay for professional advice; and it is easy to understand that as soon as it is known that any one can obtain assistance gratuitously from the Police Physician, no one will pay for such assistance. Hence has arisen a very unsatisfactory state of things. The Police Physicians complain that they are very inadequately paid for work which occupies nearly all their time, and on the other hand it is urged that many of them are men of such very inferior standing in their profession that their services are over remunerated at the low rates accorded to them. The fact is that, whether mainly in consequence of the mischievous exuberance of State charity or not, both in the country districts and in the towns the poorer classes have been so demoralised that, with the exception of the few who have the confidence of well-to-do patients, doctors find it difficult to obtain an independent living in Malta; and therefore all are eager to be subsidised by the Government, and nearly all dissatisfied that the subsidy is not greater than it is.

Proposed Reduction in the Number of Police Physicians;

178. I should have no hesitation in proposing that the staff of Police Physicians should be abolished altogether, were it not that the Government appears to be committed to its present system of medical charity, and that, were that charity suddenly withdrawn, a large part of the population would find itself without any medical assistance at all. The best way out of the difficulty, as it seems to me, therefore, is to employ as few Police Physicians as possible and to increase their rate of pay. I have ascertained from the Chief Police Physician that in his opinion the number may be reduced from twenty-eight to sixteen, whom he would distribute as follows; two in Valletta, two in Cospicua, and one each in Città Vecchia, Zebbug, Birchircara, Misida, San Giuseppe, Luca, Nasciar, Melleha, Zurrico, and Zeitun, all in Malta, together with two at Rabato and Nadur in Gozo.* *See map, facing p. 8.* The aggregate salaries of the twenty-eight now employed, including house-allowance to one, amount to £1194. I propose that the total be increased to £1300, and divided between sixteen Physicians at the places named above, in such a way as the local authorities may deem most equitable, merely suggesting that, with my insufficient knowledge of the necessities and conditions of each case, it appears to me that it may be perhaps expedient to assign £100 to the Physician at Melleha, as there his chances of obtaining private practice are very small indeed, and to allow £80 a year to each of the other fifteen.

and alteration of their Title to City and District Officers.

179. The designation of these professional employés of the Government should, I think, be altered from Police Physicians to City or District Medical Officers. Their connection with the Police and the Magistrates should be so far retained as to secure their services, whenever necessary, in furthering the ends of justice, but for all administrative purposes they should be subject to the Controller of Charitable Institutions, to whom indeed they are already formally responsible as regards the medicines supplied to them and the dispensaries under their care.

The Chief Police Physician and Chief Sanitary Officer.

180. It is doubtless necessary that the services of the Chief Police Physician should be retained until the time arrives for his retirement. This gentleman draws a fixed salary of £240, made up of £205 as Chief Police Physician and Inspector of Dispensaries, and £35 as Medical Inspector of Addolorata Cemetery. He also receives a travelling allowance of £30, and in his temporary capacity of Chief Sanitary Officer he receives another allowance of £60. His attention appears to be so entirely absorbed by sanitary and quarantine duties that he practically has little or nothing to do with the Physicians placed under his control, or with the dispensaries he is supposed to inspect. I propose, therefore, that, for the present at any rate, he be relieved of these responsibilities, and that, as long as the Sanitary Board continues, he be expected to devote himself especially, in addition to his quarantine duties, to the work connected with it, of which I presume that the inspection of the Addolorata Cemetery will form a part. If, without establishing a precedent for his successor, should one have to be appointed, he retain his present fixed salary of £240 as Chief Sanitary Officer instead of as Chief Police Physician, the Government will save the temporary allowances of £60 and £30 which he now receives.

The Sanitary Office.

181. The Sanitary Office, which owes its origin to the demand for improved drainage and other sanitary reforms in Malta, has been in existence for about three years, its expenses being met by supplementary votes in Council, of which one for the "establishment" of the current year, amounting to £690, exclusive of contingencies, which will be heavy and various, was passed last January. In the interests of public health and comfort, some organisation of the sort is doubtless necessary, but it is to be hoped that, if it becomes permanent, great care will be taken to prevent its being converted into an unnecessarily heavy and cumbersome burden on the already overtaxed resources of the

Island exchequer. With a view to economy I recommend that, until its ultimate position can be defined, it be annexed to the Department of Charitable Institutions, with which it has considerable affinity, and that the Controller be specially charged with the duty of keeping down its expenses as much as possible. *The Charitable Institutions.*

182. Its present temporary establishment consists of the Chief Sanitary Officer referred to; an Assistant Sanitary Officer, who draws £40 in addition to his allowance as Police Physician in Valletta; a Sanitary Inspector, who draws £100 in addition to his stipend as a Professor in the University; a Chemist, at £40, who is also a Professor in the University; an Engineer, at £40, who is also a Professor in the University; an Assistant Engineer, at £70; a Clerk, who draws £20 in addition to his salary in the Charitable Institutions Department; four Overseers, whose aggregate salaries amount to £190; and thirteen Sanitary Officers, who receive £10 apiece, or £130 in all, in addition to their allowances as Police Physicians. A sum of £30 is also allowed for the payment of 10s. apiece to the members of the Sanitary Board whenever they attend its meetings. *Its Staff.*

183. Here are rather more than the germs of a very large and costly addition to the number of Government Departments. The inordinate growth of this body should be restrained by all legitimate means. I am not in a position to say whether it is necessary that as many as three Professors of the University should be upon its staff, but, if so, it appears to me that the honorarium to the Sanitary Inspector, assisted as he is by two other medical men in Valletta, need not be more than is paid to the Chemist and the Engineer, or £40 instead of £100. While allowing the additional £40 allowed to the District Medical Officer who assists the Chief Sanitary Officer in managing the establishment, moreover, I think that the increased stipends accorded to the other City and District Medical Officers should suffice for all the sanitary work they have to do in addition to their other duties. If, as I have proposed, a Clerk, brought from the Police Department to the Charitable Institutions, be lent to the Sanitary Office, the £20 now paid for clerical assistance can also be saved. As all alterations to buildings, drains and the like, ordered by the sanitary authorities, ought to be executed under the direction of the Superintendent of Public Works, the employment of Overseers by the Chief Sanitary Officer, at a charge of £190 a year, should not be allowed. Whatever work of that nature has to be done would probably be done much more economically through the agency of the Public Works Department. At any rate, the other changes I have suggested will effect a reduction of £270 on the estimated expenditure of £690 a year for the "provisional and temporary" establishment of the Sanitary Office. *Proposed Reductions.*

184. Among the incidental expenses lavishly incurred by this *enfant terrible* among the organisations for spending money in Malta, I may mention that the fortnightly and annual mortality returns published in the *Government Gazette*, and reproduced with copious additions in bulky "Annual Reports," appear to me to be far in excess of the necessities of the population, and very unprofitable contributions to hygienic literature. *Mortality Returns.*

THE MONTE DI PIETA AND SAVINGS-BANK.

185. The establishment for lending money at a low rate of interest upon the security of property given in pawn, known as the Monte di Pietà, which was formerly included among the Charitable Institutions, and which is still under the supervision of the Commissioners of Charity, is now combined with that of the Government Savings-Bank; and, on account of the facilities afforded by it for this service, it also acts as custodian of the various articles, exclusive of the recognised currency, which are lodged with the Registrars of the Civil, Commercial, and other Courts, in respect of disputed claims. *The Monte di Pietà and Savings-Bank.*

186. These duties are performed by a Commissary in Valletta, with a salary of £240 a year; a Deputy Commissary in Gozo, whose remuneration for this work is included in his stipend as Deputy Collector of Land Revenue; seven Clerks, whose aggregate salaries amount to £595 a year; four Keepers and Assistant Keepers of Pledges, receiving in all £315 a year; four Appraisers of Pledges, drawing between them £150; and eight Messengers, Porters and Serjants, whose wages amount to £225; making, with £57 for contingencies, a total of £1582 a year. *Its Staff.*

187. The pawnbroking business—the extent of which may be learnt from the fact that in 1877 as many as 49,097 various articles were taken in pledge for £36,622 1s. 6d. —appears, as far as my necessarily very limited examination enabled me to judge, to be carefully and systematically conducted. As the interest at 5 per cent. paid on these and previous deposits, amounting to £2061 18s. 1d. in 1877, more than covered the entire working expenses of the establishment, including the portion devoted to Savings-Bank and other duties, it is evidently a self-supporting business. *The Monte di Pietà.*

<small>THE MONTE DI PIETA AND SAVINGS-BANK.</small>

<small>Proposed Safeguards.</small>

188. Seeing what risk is incurred in the custody of so much property, I do not think the proposal sometimes made for reducing the rate of interest is a prudent one; but it might be well to adopt the Commissary's suggestion that additional safeguards should be adopted even at some increase of expense for its protection, and that the allowances to the Appraisers of gold, silver, and jewels offered in pledge, considering the responsible nature of their duties, should be slightly augmented.

<small>Proposed Transfer of Court Deposits in Sicilian Dollars to the Treasury.</small>

189. I also think it would be expedient to lessen the Commissary's responsibility by assigning to the Receiver-General, instead of to him, the custody of such Court deposits as consist of Sicilian dollars and other foreign coin. Deposits in English currency are now lodged in the Treasury, while those composed of jewellery and precious metals are placed in the Monte di Pietà. Sicilian dollars, not being legally current in the Island, are regarded merely as securities and classed with jewellery. As, however, they unfortunately still form the principal circulating medium in the small trade of the population, and can be misappropriated with less risk of detection than trinkets and other ornaments, the strong vault of the Treasury seems to me the most convenient receptacle for them.

<small>The Savings-Bank.</small>

190. I have no suggestions to offer as regards the Savings-Bank business, which appears to be carried on in an altogether satisfactory way, with advantage both to the depositors, whose accumulated savings amounted to £213,133 at the close of 1877, and to the Government, which invests the greater portion of this money in Consols.

THE PUBLIC LIBRARIES.

<small>THE PUBLIC LIBRARIES.</small>

191. An estimated expenditure of £356 a year is incurred on account of the salary of the principal of the Public Library and Museum in Valletta, a small honorarium to the officiating librarian at Gozo, the wages of three porters, and certain incidental expenses; and a sum of £300, including the interest of a bequest of £800, is annually voted for the purchase of books and objects. This money is spent by the Librarians under the direction of a Library Committee.

<small>Proposed Transfer of Archives from the Public Registry.

* See par. 213.</small>

192. If the suggestion I shall make as to the transference to the Public Library in Valletta of the historical and antiquarian documents now retained in the Public Registry* be adopted, the manuscript treasures of this repository will be greatly augmented, and arrangements may be made, as in the case of larger establishments of the same kind in other countries, for enabling literary inquirers to make use of them under the immediate inspection of the Librarian. By such a transfer the documents will be rendered more accessible to students, and the clerks in the Public Registry will be relieved of duties and responsibilities which, though they do not now press heavily upon them, are alien to their proper functions. If these documents were kept under lock and key, and only allowed to be examined in the Librarian's own room by persons furnished with a permit from the Chief Secretary, for which a small fee of say 6d. might be charged, their safety would be as complete as at present.

<small>Proposed Improvements in the Custody of the Library.</small>

193. Complaints are made as to the decay of many of the books in the Library from moth and dust, in consequence of insufficiency of attendants. If, in the opinion of the Library Committee, these complaints are well founded, it would be well to employ in this establishment at any rate one of the redundant messengers in the Departments which I propose to re-organise, leaving it to be decided, when vacancies occur, whether it is expedient permanently to enlarge the establishment.

THE GOVERNMENT PRINTING OFFICE.

<small>THE GOVERNMENT PRINTING OFFICE.</small>

194. A fixed charge of £690 is made in the Annual Estimates for the salaries of the Superintendent of the Government Printing Office, who is also custodian of stationery, and of the seven Compositors, the four Pressmen, and the Distributor of the *Government Gazette*, employed by him. In addition to this amount, provision is made in the regular Estimates for £260 a year, on account of "Extra Pressmen, Apprentices, &c., when required," which was in 1877 exceeded by £114 1s. 5d., making an expenditure altogether of £1064 1s. 5d. In this sum no account is taken of the paper used in the printing establishment, as that is supplied by the several Departments on whose behalf the work is done. In the Estimates for 1879 a total of £736 is provided for stationery,

besides about £90 out of the £250 voted for expenses in connection with the Council of Government. If to all these items be added £53 allowed for the cost of printing materials, it appears that more than £1900 a year is annually expended by the Government on account of printing and stationery. THE GOVERN-
MENT PRINT-
ING OFFICE.

195. As far back as 1837 the special commissioners appointed at that time to inquire into the affairs of Malta condemned the existence of the Government Printing Office, and recommended its abolition at an early date, on the ground that about £790 were spent on the salaries of persons employed in printing which was worth only £209. The excessive cost of this establishment was again pointed out by Mr. Rowsell in 1877. The existence of a large and permanent staff of compositors and others, and the possession of extensive plant, render it easy for a great deal of useless or almost useless printing work to be done, and that which is necessary is inevitably far more costly than it would be if executed under a duly prepared contract with one or more of the private printing establishments in the Colony. Its Extravagance.

196. I should have no hesitation in proposing that this office be at once dispensed with altogether, were it not that the local authorities consider it important to have at their disposal the means of from time to time printing documents which it is not desirable to bring within reach of the public. As to the reality of this alleged necessity I can form no opinion; but, assuming it to be the case, I see no reason for maintaining so large an establishment as now exists. I therefore recommend that the supernumerary pressmen and others, who are not entitled to pensions, be at once discharged; that no allowance for extra work be made to the men on the fixed establishment; and that gradually, as they reach the age proper for retirement, their numbers be reduced, until there remain at any rate no more than three compositors and two pressmen, with a man or boy to distribute the *Gazette* and perform the other duties of a messenger. On the retirement of the present Superintendent, moreover, I consider that a salary of £90 or £100 a year will amply remunerate such an official as may be needed to act as foreman of the printing office and custodian of stationery. I also propose that, except on such rare occasions of necessity as may arise for obtaining fresh type and repairing the presses, no further expense be incurred on account of plant until it has been brought down to the actual requirements of the office. By this means an immediate reduction of at least £200 can be made in the amount provided for in the Estimates, even if an additional allowance of £100 be necessary to cover such outside printing work as has to be done by contract, and it is not unreasonable to expect that the ultimate saving will be not less than £500 or £600 a year. Proposed Reductions.

197. With the proposed reduction of the resources of the Government Printing Office, it will, of course, be requisite to have a certain quantity of printing executed in private establishments. If this is properly contracted for, however, and if due care is taken to see that no unnecessary work is done, great economy cannot fail to result. As the existing appliances of the Government Office are specially adapted for producing the numerous forms required by the various Departments, the Blue-book (in the contracted form which I shall suggest),* and the *Government Gazette*, I propose that all such work, as well as the printing of any confidential matter that may be called for, shall be retained in the office, the spare time of the employés being devoted to whatever miscellaneous printing may be necessary, and that the rest, including especially the reports of debates in the Council of Government and other publications connected therewith, shall be, as far as is necessary, executed elsewhere. At present no record is kept in the office of the time and labour spent on the various jobs performed in it, so that it is impossible to ascertain the exact cost of any one of them. If that cost were known, it would probably lead to economy. As regards the reports of the debates of Council, published in what is known as the local "Hansard" especially, of which 75 copies are printed and perhaps 20 or 25 copies distributed, it is only reasonable to suppose that, if the members of the Council were aware that the expense per copy of each volume, including the stenographer's salary, is at least £3 or £4, they would forego the luxury of seeing their speeches printed in such fulness as is denied even to the members of the British Houses of Parliament. Proposed
Employment
of Outside
Printers.

* See par. 28

The Local
"Hansard."

198. By the time when the gradual reduction of the Government Printing Establishment, which I propose, is effected, I hope that it will be found expedient to dispense with it altogether. In anticipation of that, I recommend that, if it is necessary to make any new appointments to it, they should be only temporary, not entitling their holders to pension. Such an arrangement would in any case be preferable to the present one. It is idle to expect rapid and efficient work from compositors and printers who know not only that, whether they work or not, they are sure of holding their appointments for life, but also that by prolonging their work beyond the official hours they can secure an addition to their income in the shape of "extra pay." Possible extinction of the Establishment.

THE GOVERN-
MENT PRINT-
ING OFFICE.

Bookbinding.

* See par. 268.

Proposed Sub-
ordination of
the Establish-
ment to the
Chief Secre-
tary's Office.

199. To each Department an allowance is now made in the Estimates for bookbinding, and this work is separately arranged for in the different offices. Considerable economy could be effected if all the bookbinding required to be done by the several Departments were executed in the Archives branch of the General Registry of the Courts, which already has appliances for binding legal documents.*

200. In order to secure all the economies and reforms that may be effected in this establishment, the general superintendence and control of its arrangements, which now devolves on the Chief Secretary, should be much more careful and complete than it has hitherto been; but I do not consider that the efficient performance of this duty ought to occupy more than a third or a quarter of the time of one able and conscientious Clerk.

THE POST OFFICE.

THE POST
OFFICE.

Imperial
Charges.

Local
Charges.

Proposed
Transfer of
the whole
Establish-
ment to the
Local Govern-
ment.

201. The Post Office in Malta is, in the main, a branch establishment of the General Post Office in London, which provides the salaries of the Postmaster, five Clerks, a Sorter, a Messenger, and four Letter Carriers, amounting, with incidental expenses, to about £1600 a year. It also provides for the conveyance of all English and foreign mails to and from Valletta—except that £880 out of the £2080 paid for the Messina and Malta service is drawn from local funds; and on the other hand it appropriates all the revenue derived from the sale of British stamps and other postal charges. For the services rendered by the Post Office employés in connection with the Island postal service the local Government adds £212 to their Imperial salaries, and provides and keeps in repair the premises occupied by them, receiving for the same a rent of £50 a year. It also spends, according to the Annual Estimates, about £270 on the conveyance and delivery of letters to the country districts of Malta and Gozo, in addition to the £880 mentioned above; while, as a partial set-off to these charges, it derives about £140 a year from the sale of Island postage-stamps. Thus the net cost of the Post Office to Malta exceeds £1150 a year.

202. A strong desire is expressed by the local Government for the transference to it of the larger share in the establishment now held by the Imperial authorities, and it appears to me that that course, besides being in harmony with the arrangements existing in nearly every other British colony and dependency, would be attended by considerable advantage. The arrangement of details must depend upon more formal communications than I am at present in a position to make with the authorities of the General Post Office and Her Majesty's Treasury; but from information I have obtained since my return to England, it appears to me probable that matters may be adjusted in the way which I shall roughly sketch out. In the event of the Government of Malta taking entire charge of the Post Office, it will have, in accordance with the terms of the Postal Union, to pay for the transit of letters from the Island through Italy (including one sea-service a week between Malta and Messina, which is provided for by the Italian Government) and France, which, if the postage of 1877-8 represents the average, may be estimated at £650 a year. The General Post Office also proposes to claim the full postal rate chargeable on Malta letters distributed in or passing through the United Kingdom, which in 1877-8 amounted to about £1500. The subsidy paid to the Peninsular and Oriental Steam Navigation Company for the conveyance of mails to and from the East, I am informed, is—and under the new arrangements to be entered upon in 1880 will continue to be—greatly in excess of the value of the postage charged on the letters thus conveyed; but it may be expected that the General Post Office will, as regards this item, consent to do for Malta what it now does for many other colonies, i.e., accept the full amount of postage levied on such letters, which may be estimated at £150 a year, in satisfaction of its claim for the cost of their transmission. The General Post Office also appears willing to contribute £600 a year, being the estimated surplus revenue derived from letters sent from the United Kingdom to Malta viâ Italy, towards the expense of maintaining a second weekly service between Malta and Messina, for which the Government of Malta now pays £2080 a year to the Florio Company, receiving £1200 from the Imperial Government. Assuming that the same expense, or £1480 a year, continues to be incurred for a second weekly service, and that the other charges are as I have stated, the total amount which will, probably, have to be paid by the Malta Government for the conveyance of mails may be assumed to be about £3780 a year. It will also have, of course, under the proposed arrangement, to defray all the cost of the Post Office establishment, including the distribution of letters throughout Malta and Gozo and other miscellaneous expenses. These charges now amounting to about £2080, of which nearly £1600 is paid from Imperial and about £480 from local sources, appear to me to be excessive. If the

35

successor to the present Postmaster is chosen from the natives of Malta, he may be amply remunerated by less than half the emoluments which are now assigned to the post, and which far exceed those of every other civil servant in the Island except the Chief Secretary, not excluding even the President of the Court of Appeal. The present large staff of clerks and subordinates also seems to be capable of reduction. If the present outlay of about £2080 on account of the establishment and incidental expenses be reduced to about £1520, as I think it may, the total cost of the Malta Post Office may be estimated at about £5300 a year. As the revenue in 1877–8, including £140 derived from the sale of Island postage-stamps, amounted to nearly £5800, it is thus probable that, besides collateral advantages, a profit of something like £500 a year may be expected should the Post Office be transferred from Imperial to local control, instead of a deficit as at present of about £1150.* This advantage, however, will be more than neutralised, if the Government enters into arrangements, as it proposes, for adding to its present number of two mails a week *via* Italy.

The Post Office.

THE PUBLIC REGISTRY.

203. In this Department the Archivist and Notary to Government—who as such is nominally included in the Chief Secretary's Department, with a salary of £200—officiates as Registrar of Hypothecations, with an addition of £80 to his salary; and has under him an Assistant-Registrar and six Clerks, whose salaries amount to £655 a year; while an allowance of £20 for "extra clerical assistance," £50 for the wages of two Messengers, and £98 for stationery, bookbinding, and petty expenses, raise the total to £1103. Such an establishment ought to be at least self-supporting; but it earns only about £650 a year in the shape of fees, and thus costs, irrespective of pensions, about £450 a year.

The Public Registry.

204. As Notary, the head of this Department prepares all Government contracts, leases, and similar documents. As Registrar, he records all hypothecations or mortgages, all "insinuazioni" or transfers of property, and all acts of civil status or entries of births, deaths and marriages. As Archivist, he has custody of all the records appertaining to his office, as well as of an important collection of legal and miscellaneous documents, illustrating the history of the Knights of St. John, and of Malta under their rule, copies or extracts from which he has to furnish when required for antiquarian or other researches.

Its various Functions.

205. The Department thus labours under the disadvantage of having assigned to it various functions which, if not altogether inharmonious, are more likely to be satisfactorily performed if they are kept apart. The fact that, not only the head of the establishment, but also four of his subordinates, are notaries entitled to augment their official incomes by private practice, moreover, is calculated to stand in the way of the efficient performance of public business.

---

* The following is an approximate estimate of the revenue and expenditure of the Malta Post Office in accordance with the plan sketched out above. The credits are, in round numbers, the amounts actually received in 1877–8, and will probably be exceeded, as the postal business of the Island appears to be steadily increasing. In that case, however, a proportionate increase in the charges must be looked for.

Revenue.	£	Expenditure.		£	£
Sale of Postage Stamps	5,170	Establishment:—			
Collections on Unpaid Correspondence	260	Postmaster		300	
Private Box Fees	70	Four Clerks, £60 to £250 (see Par. 294), say		620	
Commission on Money Orders	300	Sorters, Letter Carriers, Messengers, &c., say (present outlay)		440	
		Incidental Expenses (ditto)		160	1,520
		Conveyance of Mails:—			
		Subsidy to Florio Company	2,080		
		Less Imperial Contribution	600		
				1,480	
		Foreign Countries, for Land Transport		650	
		British Inland Rates		1,500	
		Sea Postage on P. & O. Mails		150	3,780
					5,300
		Balance			500
	£5,800				£5,800

It should be added that, if the Post Office be transferred to the Local Government, the latter will be expected to contribute its share towards the pensions of the employés now in the service who come under the provisions of the Superannuation Acts, the Imperial Government paying only such proportions of the pensions as accrue for the periods during which those employés have been in its service.

THE PUBLIC REGISTRY.

Proposed Employment of an independent Government Notary.

206. The work of the Notary to Government should, I have no hesitation in saying, be assigned to an independent professional man of good repute in the Island. All contracts entered into, or leases granted, by the Government should be prepared by this Notary, the contractors or lessees bearing the expenses both of the originals and of so many copies and translations into Italian as it may be agreed upon that either party is entitled to. This system is now followed by the Imperial Government in Malta, and is found to work well. As Government contracts are generally for periods of not less than one year, and leases extend over from one to ninety-nine years, the cost to each individual would be so trifling that no increase of prices or diminution of rent would result from the transfer of these charges from the Government to the contractor or lessee, while sales of real property would not, of course, be affected by the change. Seeing, however, that the Government contracts alone number about 270 a year, and, with the fees for copies and translations, may on a very moderate estimate be expected to yield upwards of £500 a year, they would amply remunerate the Government Notary for his own work, and for all the clerical assistance and office accommodation he may require.

207. So long as the present Government Notary retains his office, I recommend that the ordinary notarial fees for contracts and leases be charged by him on behalf of the Government, and the proceeds duly credited in the public accounts. On his retirement the new arrangement should come into force, the whole of the notarial work of the Government being assigned to a single competent person, who should be responsible for its due execution, but who should derive all his remuneration for it from fees obtained from the public, and who should have no claim to superannuation or to employment as Government Notary for any longer period than is found advantageous to the Government.

The Registration business.

208. The registration business now done in the Public Registry is cumbered by much superfluous work which ought to be eliminated.

Civil Status Acts and Insinuazioni.

209. Instead of making complete transcripts of the acts of civil status, and of deeds of transfers, into books which are practically useless, as reference when required is invariably made to the original documents, it would be sufficient to bind the documents themselves in volumes, each bearing at the end the Registrar's certificate as to the number of acts or deeds contained in it, and, by help of complete alphabetical indexes, to make references to these volumes easy.

Acts of Hypothecation.

210. Acts of hypothecation in respect of Government contracts for supplies may generally be altogether dispensed with by making it a condition of agreement that the monthly payments shall be made one month in arrear until the completion of the contract. In exceptional cases, where that form of security is not considered adequate, the contractor should be required to find two sureties for the due fulfilment of his undertaking. This simple mode of proceeding is found to be effective in other countries, and far preferable to burdening the property of a contractor with what is equivalent to a mortgage.

211. Acts of hypothecation on behalf of the public must necessarily continue to be registered; but I believe that many beneficial and labour-saving reforms can easily be devised by the intelligent employés in this Department. The form of the unwieldy and half blank registers now in use, for example, may be altered with great advantage. Alterations may also be made in what is styled the "registry of references," which, I am led to believe, is rather a measure of private convenience to practising notaries than one that properly devolves on the Government to keep. It is yet more important that some arrangement should be arrived at for treating as lapsed, hypothecations which have not been renewed during a given period, say thirty years, as in Italy and France. Much time is wasted in the Public Registry in searching through old registers and giving extracts from them, and general certificates based upon them, which a very simple alteration of the law might obviate. These are matters on which I do not feel competent to offer any precise schemes, but I recommend the appointment of a committee, from which notaries, excepting one or two of those employed in this Department, should be excluded, to determine what reforms may be effected without detriment to the public.

Proposed transfer of the Registration work to the Chief Registrar;

212. The duties proper to the Public Registry, if that course be adopted, will, I am convinced, be so much reduced that there will be no necessity for maintaining it as a separate establishment. There would, on the other hand, be great economy to the Government and convenience to the public in amalgamating it with the registration branches of the Law Courts. I therefore recommend that the Public Registry, as a separate office, be abolished, and that so much of its business, all more or less of a legal character, as is not provided for by assigning the notarial work of the Government to an independent Notary, be placed under the direction of the Chief Registrar, to whose duties and responsibilities I shall refer in a later portion of this Report.*

* See par. 251.

213. I have already suggested the transference to the Public Library of that portion of the Archives which is especially of historical and antiquarian value, as their present repository is most unsuitable and most inconvenient as a place of reference, both to their custodians and to strangers who wish to examine them.* The rest of the Archives will naturally follow the registration business, and be suitably placed with the other legal documents at present assigned to the two Archivists, of whom one is established within the precincts of the Courts, while the other has charge of the notarial acts preserved in the Auberge d'Italie.† THE PUBLIC REGISTRY.
and of the Archives to the Public Library and the Archives of the Courts.
* See par. 192.
† See par. 26т.

214. By the arrangements I have sketched out, the services of at least one Clerk or of the Assistant-Registrar may be dispensed with on account of the notarial work being removed from the office; and for the reformed duties of registration and records which I propose to transfer to the clerical service of the Courts, I anticipate that an Assistant-Registrar and three Clerks will amply suffice. A prospective saving on the establishment of the salaries of the Registrar and Notary, the Assistant-Registrar, two Clerks, and two Messengers, of, including extra clerical assistance and contingencies, at least £700 a year may be counted upon; in addition to which, the building now used for the Public Registry will be available for other purposes. Consequent Savings.

THE INFERIOR COURTS.

215. With a population of about 152,000, including 151 Advocates, 88 Legal Procurators, and 69 Notaries, the islands of Malta and Gozo are provided with five Superior Courts, in which six Judges sit, with four Courts of Judicial Police, giving occupation to eight Magistrates, with seven Syndics' Courts, each having its own Syndic, and with the following number of subordinate employés:—sixteen Registrars, five Assistant-Registrars, four Reporters, two Archivists of Notarial Acts, one Computist, twenty-one Clerks, ten Copyists, two Interpreters, seven Marshals, two Guardians, thirteen Porters, six Messengers, and one Regulator of the Court clock. One Keeper of Archives, four Clerks, two Bookbinders, and one Fatigue man, though not forming part of the fixed establishment, are regularly employed in the Record Branch of the Superior Courts. There are also in Malta a Crown Advocate, with his Messenger, and an Advocate for the Poor; and in Gozo an Assistant Crown Advocate and Advocate for the Poor. The cost of these hundred and twenty-three functionaries, of sundry clerical and other assistance, and of various allowances and contingencies, as shown in the Annual Estimates, amounts to £15,631 a year. The revenue which should have been received in 1877 from fines, forfeitures and fees of Court was £5786; so that the net expenditure on account of the administration of justice, without including pensions and buildings, is nearly £10,000 a year. THE INFERIOR COURTS.
The Judicial and Magisterial Establishments of Malta.

216. In the remarks I shall offer under this head I shall confine myself to the pointing out of what appear to me to be defects, and what I consider to be possible improvements, in the machinery of the Superior and Inferior Courts, without entering into any examination of strictly legal questions. Technical matters are beyond my province; but no technical knowledge is requisite to see that this machinery is far more elaborate and cumbersome than it need be, and that any improvement that can be effected in it must be of great advantage to a community which, one of the poorest in the British dominions, is unusually prone to increase its poverty by litigation, under the encouragement of the Government, and at the instigation of an inordinate number of professional men eagerly competing with one another for a scanty livelihood.

217. As regards the Syndics, it must be borne in mind that their duties are by no means exclusively concerned with the administration of justice. They are, in their several districts, representatives of the Government in all its functions. Successors, in great measure, of the "Luogotenenti" or "capi dei casali," who were instituted in 1798, except that their main qualifications were to be legal rather than military, the "sindaci," who were called into existence in 1839, were intended to perform various duties besides those of country magistrates, which had grown in importance after the suppression, in 1822, of the country Police Court at Città Vecchia or Notabile, the ancient capital of the island. In each of the seven districts into which Malta was divided† an Advocate was appointed to act as Syndic, with duties thus officially described in 1848; "(1) As Civil Magistrate, to hear and determine, in a summary way, all civil causes not exceeding the amount of £2 1s. 8d., when the defendant is resident The Syndics: their Origin and Duties.
† See map, facing p. 8.

The Interior Courts. within his district. (2) As Officer of Police, to attend to the conservation of the peace within the limits of his district, and to the apprehension and detention of offenders. (3.) As Head of the District, to report immediately all extraordinary occurrences to Government; to make weekly and monthly reports on the state of his district, and a detailed report, every six months, stating the actual population, the cultivation and produce of lands, &c. He is also to watch over the markets; inspect from time to time all scales, weights and measures; and report any contravention of the market regulations to the Inspector of Police. He is, moreover, to be careful that the streets of the casals in his district, and the roads around them, are kept clear of building materials, &c." The duties then assigned to the Syndic have been continued, with some modifications, to the present day. By the "Laws of Organisation and Civil Procedure" passed in 1854, the Syndic's power in civil matters now extends to £5, and is coequal with that of a City Magistrate, when sitting alone, though appeal from his decisions, as from those of a single City Magistrate, lies to three City Magistrates, " when constituted as a Court of secondary instance." By the " Criminal Code " of 1854, and some subsequent ordinances, he is enabled to punish, with fine and detention, gamblers, vagabonds and mendicants, parents neglecting their children, and owners of vicious dogs; but in the case of more serious misdemeanours he can only make preliminary inquiries and send the supposed offenders for examination to Valletta. He is not only, within his district, the senior Police Officer, and the representative of the Land Revenue and Public Works Department, but an important part of his duty has to do with the distribution of alms and other sorts of charitable relief in connection with the Department of Charitable Institutions. Perhaps, however, his most valuable duties are those, not easily to be defined, of a quasi-patriarchal nature, as the protector and adviser of his village neighbours on all family matters and in all petty disputes in which the parish priest is not regarded as a more satisfactory referee. It is chiefly on account of the manifest inexpediency of depriving the country districts of such amiable and intelligent "heads of the villages" as the Syndics generally appear to be, and of the difficulty of providing in a less expensive way for the various duties performed by them in connection with police discipline, charity, public works, &c., that I abstain from recommending any considerable reduction in their numbers.

Proposed extension of their Magisterial Powers, and change in their Title. 218. If the Syndicates are to be maintained, however, it seems to me very desirable that the magisterial powers of the Syndics should be enlarged. I propose, indeed, that the term Syndic shall be abolished and that of District Magistrate be substituted for it, the cumbrous title of Magistrate of Judicial Police being also displaced by that of City Magistrate, so that the differences now existing between the two classes of Magistrates may be as far as possible removed. The District Magistrate will necessarily have many extra-judicial duties to perform, and his strictly magisterial work will happily be, as a rule, very light; but it will be in many ways advantageous that his position and dignity as a Magistrate should be strengthened, and that he should be enabled, if he desires it, to look forward to promotion from his rural office to a more important post in the capital.

The Magistrates of Judicial Police. 219. There are at present five Magistrates of Judicial Police in Malta, two of whom sit every day to hear criminal cases in Valletta, while one goes on alternate days to what is known as the Court of the Three Cities, at Cospicua, on the other side of the Grand Harbour. In the Civil Court at Valletta, as a rule, one of them sits twice a week for ordinary cases; and on two other days, when necessary, appeal cases are heard, as prescribed by law, before a Court of three.

The Syndics' and Magistrates' Courts. 220. The Syndics in the seven country districts, each comprising from two or three to five or six casals, and having their several headquarters at Città Vecchia, Zebbug, Birchircara, Nasciar, Curmi, Zurrico, and Zeitun, with an aggregate population of about 72,000, now deal with civil cases in which not more than £5 is involved, and with some of the most insignificant of the police offences, known as "contraventions." The Court of the Three Cities deals with civil cases up to £5, and with all ordinary police offences occurring among a population of about 26,000, as well as with the more serious cases in the two adjoining Syndicates, with a population of about 24,000, which the Syndics are not allowed to dispose of. The Valletta Court deals with all police cases, both civil and criminal, arising among the 35,000 inhabitants of Valletta and Floriana, and with the serious offences coming from the 48,000 inhabitants of the five other Syndicates; and the Valletta Magistrates also hold a Court of Second Instance for hearing any appeals that may be made in civil cases from their own Courts of First Instance or from the Syndics' Courts. Some of these arrangements are attended with great inconvenience, and I anticipate considerable economy to the Government, and yet more important advantages to the public, from the changes which I shall propose, and nearly all of which have received the sanction of the learned President of the Court of Appeal, who is the chief judicial officer of the Crown in Malta.* THE INFERIOR COURTS.

221. As the Syndics are all required to be Advocates by profession, and were chosen from the same class which supplies the Courts of Valletta with Magistrates and Judges, I am of opinion that their powers should be so far enlarged as to enable them to deal, not only with a few minor contraventions, but with all such police cases as come within the jurisdiction of the City Magistrates. Taking the average of the past three years, I find that about 2800 alleged offenders are annually sent up from the seven Syndics' Courts to be examined in Valletta or the Three Cities. Assuming that, on an average, only two witnesses are required in each case, and I am told that the number often rises to four or five, there are thus no fewer than 8400 persons, including the policemen in charge of the accused, brought up from distances of one to seven miles to assist in the hearing of these 2800 cases, after which they have to trudge home again. Often the cases are adjourned, and then the process has to be gone through a second or perhaps even a third time. In the event of the accused being convicted, moreover, if his offence deserves more than the three days' detention permitted in the small Valletta Prison, he has to be conducted by a policeman to Corradino, which is probably nearer to every one of the Syndics' Courts than either the Valletta or the Three Cities' Court. These facts will show how much time, labour, and money are wasted, in the case of policemen, witnesses and innocent persons, as well as of the small offenders themselves, by the present arrangements. If the police were empowered to bring persons suspected of contraventions and minor offences before the District Magistrates, the cases would generally be disposed of in a few hours, or even less, so that, at the outside, prisoners need not be detained over more than one night in the district lock-ups, and immense advantage would result to all the parties concerned. As the Syndics would have the power of committing to Valletta Prison, or to the Corradino, as the case might require, and as is now done by the City Magistrates, the trouble of bringing even condemned persons to Valletta would be spared whenever the punishment prescribed should exceed three days' detention.

* See Appendix C. (I).
Inconvenience of present arrangements as regards Police Offences.

Proposed increase of the District Magistrates' Authority.

222. In accordance with that proposed extension of the Syndics' power, I further recommend the adoption of the President's suggestions, both that District Magistrates be authorised to hold such inquests or inquiries within their districts as are now held by City Magistrates, and also that they be charged with the inspection of all notarial acts drawn up by notaries residing in their districts.†

† See Appendix C. (I).

223. I am also of opinion that the "Laws of Organisation and Civil Procedure" should be so far altered as to abolish the right of appeal against the decisions of either City or District Magistrates in all cases where the amounts involved do not exceed £2. I find that, in 1877, 194 such cases were brought before the Magistrates' Court of Second Instance in Valletta, of which 58 were "ceded, abandoned or adjusted," 99 decided, and 37 left over to the following year. Though hardly credible, it is a fact that appeals are now sometimes made for sums as low as one *scudo*, or 1s. 8d., and encouragement is given to such frivolous cases by frequently allowing the appellants to occupy the time of the Court and its officers free of charge, inasmuch as, the fees of Court not being exacted in advance, it is a common occurrence for them never to be paid at all. For criminal or police offences Magistrates are empowered to condemn culprits to fines of £5, or three months' imprisonment, without right of appeal; while in these petty civil cases, where no question of law is involved, the judgment of one Magistrate is not held sufficient to decide a case for a few shillings. In an island so oversupplied with lawyers as Malta, it is hardly surprising that efforts of all sorts should be made to promote litigation, but it appears to me to be the duty of the Government, in the interests of the unfortunate suitors themselves, most decidedly to discourage such practices. I feel assured that the limit I have named might, with great advantage to all but advocates and procurators, be increased to £5, and I only abstain from recommending that sum as a limit in deference to opinions expressed to me by professional men, that the final disposal of such cases in District Courts might deprive suitors of counsel's assistance, because of the time that would be occupied in going to them from Valletta as well as the loss of dignity that an advocate's appearance there might bring to him. Without venturing to deny these assumptions, I find it difficult to conceive any lack of legal assistance when the most remote of the District Courts is less than seven miles from the headquarters of the profession, and when lawyers are so numerous that they are eager to espouse causes in which their benighted clients contend over again for sums as small as a single *scudo*.

Proposed withdrawal of Right of Appeal in Civil Cases below £2.

224. In addition to thus limiting the right of appeal against a Magistrate's decision to £2, I recommend that all appeals for sums above that amount should be sent direct to Her Majesty's Court of Appeal, where, as I shall presently point out, they can be

Proposed Abolition of the Magistrates' Civil

generally dealt with by one Judge.* By this change the Magistrates' Court of Second Instance will be relieved of all its remaining duties. It may therefore be abolished, and, the necessity for three Magistrates to sit in it being removed, the number of Magistrates may be reduced from five to three.

The Inferior Courts.
Court of Second Instance.
* See par. 244.
Proposed Alteration of the Territorial Limits of Magistracies.

225. The territorial barriers between the jurisdiction of the Magistrates and that of the Syndics, however suitable they may have been when they were established, now require to be altered. The growing trade of Valletta and the Three Cities has caused a great number of persons, who would probably reside within the walls if they could, to establish themselves in the suburbs; and the surrounding casals, whose populations have greatly increased of late years, are now chiefly inhabited by men whose daily occupations are in the town and its harbours, where they are employed in coaling vessels, discharging cargoes, plying boats, driving cabs, retailing cheap commodities, &c. Such people are townsmen in all but the name, and whenever they appear in court, whether as complainants, as defendants, or as witnesses, it is on every ground more convenient that they should come before the City Magistrates than before the Syndics in whose districts they dwell. I therefore recommend that the area of the City Magistrates' jurisdiction be extended so as to take in at any rate the nearest and most important of these suburban towns and villages. Without attempting to define the limits exactly, I may specify Zabbar and Corradino Hill on the one side, and Sliema, Misida, and Pietà on the other, as places which certainly ought to be brought within the jurisdiction of the Three Cities' and the Valletta Courts respectively. The addition thus made to the City Magistrates' duties will be considerably less than the work from which I propose to relieve them by augmenting the powers of the Syndics.

Proposed Reduction in their Numbers.

226. That proposed curtailment of the districts nearest to Valletta will strengthen a suggestion I should feel justified in making in any case, to the effect that the number of country districts, as far as the Syndics' jurisdiction is concerned, should be reduced from seven to five. At present there are Syndics' Courts at Zebbug, Curmi, Birchircara, and Nasciar, forming a quadrangle of which the base measures only there miles and the other three sides less than two miles each. Two of these Courts may very easily be dispensed with, and the areas of the jurisdiction for the remaining five Syndics, to be called in future District Magistrates, should be so arranged as in the main to equalise their work and as far as possible suit the convenience of the rural population.

227. If the above proposals are adopted, there will, as vacancies occur, be a reduction of two Magistrates of Judicial Police and two Syndics; and the duties of the Inferior Courts of Malta will hereafter be performed by three City and five District Magistrates. The four supernumeraries should be transferable to either District or City Courts, as the public interests may require, until all are absorbed. After that, District Magistrates should be considered to have a claim to promotion to the City Courts, to which they should be occasionally surrogated, to supply the temporary absence of any of their colleagues. It might be well to establish a rule prescribing a triennial interchange of districts to the District Magistrates in order that there may be no risk of local associations interfering with the impartial exercise of their powers.

The Salaries of District and City Magistrates.

228. For the District Magistrates I consider that the salary of £150, with an allowance of £27 for travelling and clerical expenses, now assigned to them as Syndics, is a sufficient remuneration, especially if they have a prospect of being promoted to the City Magistracy. The salaries of the City Magistrates, however, call for some augmentation. At present, they commence at £200, rising to £220 after five, and £240 after ten years' service, the Senior Magistrate receiving a personal allowance of £70 as nominal Inspector of the Corradino Prison. For experienced professional men, possessing all the qualifications necessary for the magisterial office in the cities, these rates appear to me inadequate. I recommend that, commencing at £200, their salaries should be raised by quinquennial increments of £50 to £300, with an addition of £50 to the Senior Magistrate's salary, which should cover any extraneous services he may be required to perform. If District Magistrates are promoted, their previous service should not count for increments. An indispensable qualification for City Magistrates should be such a knowledge of English as will enable them to conduct the business of their Courts in that language.

The Magistrates' Courts in Gozo.

229. I have treated thus far only of the Magistrates and Syndics in Malta. In the Island of Gozo there are three Magistrates of Judicial Police, whose jurisdiction in civil matters is extended, with certain limitations, to include such cases as in Malta come within the competence of the First and Second Halls of the Superior Civil Court. The island being small, and its population of about 19,000 being apparently less given to litigation than their neighbours in Malta, its magisterial and judicial

business is happily very light. The cases brought before the Magistrates sitting as a Civil Court in First Instance were in 1877 less than a third as many as the similar cases in Valletta; the criminal cases brought before them were less than a twelfth as many as those heard by the Valletta Magistrates; and their labours in the way of superior jurisdiction, measured by numbers, were considerably less than an eighth as heavy as those of the Civil Court. The magisterial and judicial duties to be performed at Gozo do not therefore appear to be greater than one person should be expected to attend to. As, however, inconvenience might arise from the illness or temporary absence of a single Magistrate, I propose that in future there should be two instead of three as at present. If it is considered necessary to hold an occasional Court of three Magistrates, the gentleman who acts as Deputy Collector of Land Revenue, Deputy Controller of Charitable Institutions, and Deputy Commissary of the Monte di Pietà, and who is an Advocate by profession, might be qualified to serve also, when required, in a magisterial capacity. After the retirement of the present Senior Magistrate in Gozo, who has already been thirty-six years in the service, I propose also that the Magistrates should rank with the District Magistrates in Malta, be subject to the same triennial interchanges, have the same prospects of promotion to the City Magistracy, and, on the removal of the present functionaries, draw similar salaries and allowances, viz., £150 and £27, instead of the present scale of £180, rising to £200.

<small>THE INFERIOR COURTS.</small>

<small>Proposed changes in the Gozo Magistracies.</small>

230. The entire magisterial staff of Malta and Gozo will, if the suggestions I have made be adopted, consist hereafter of three City Magistrates and seven District Magistrates, whose aggregate emoluments will vary between a minimum of £1889 and a maximum of £2189, being a saving of from £400 to £700 a year upon the present expenditure of £2589.

<small>Economies in the Magisterial Staff.</small>

231. Other economies may be effected, and at the same time the progress of business may be facilitated, by certain changes in the clerical arrangements and in the procedure of the Courts, especially in those of Valletta, the Three Cities, and Gozo.

<small>Economies in the Clerical Arrangements.</small>

232. When the City Magistrates are now called upon to hold inquiries or inquests out of Court, they generally take with them an Assistant Registrar or Clerk to note down, under their dictation, the depositions of witnesses. This practice necessitates the maintenance of a clerical staff in excess of the ordinary wants of the office. The Magistrates, aided by the Police, should make it a rule to do always what they now only do exceptionally—that is, write the depositions themselves. The number of investigations which, under the proposed alterations in the districts, they would have to make, would be greatly reduced, and this change would involve no great labour. If, as is alleged, the handwriting of some of the Magistrates is too illegible to serve as a permanent record, while it is necessary that the original depositions should be preserved in case of being needed as legal evidence, the hieroglyphic documents might be accompanied by transcripts made by Clerks acquainted with the Magistrates' caligraphy, and certified by them, to serve hereafter as interpretations.

<small>Depositions at Inquests.</small>

233. In the Civil Court the registers of sentences, in their present form, may, in my opinion, be replaced by an improved record in the following manner;—The Magistrates' decision should be written on the back of the citation to which it refers, instead of being transcribed at length in the register. The substance of the evidence given by witnesses, now taken down in writing by the Magistrate in a rough book, should be noted by him on separate sheets of paper, and be attached to the citation, with the sentence indorsed on it, and any other documents referring to the case. These citations, sentences, and other documents, being kept in consecutive order and bound in volumes, duly indexed, would form the most complete and convenient records for future use. Much clerical labour would thus be saved, and all subsequent references to cases dealt with by the Magistrates, whether by the Court, by parties to the suits, or by other interested persons, would be greatly facilitated by all the papers being found together, instead of, as at present, inquirers having to look for the sentences in one book, for evidence in a second, and for documents elsewhere. In cases of appeal these original records might be made use of, instead of copies being taken as is now done.

<small>Registers of Sentences, &c.</small>

234. It has been suggested to me—though this is a professional question on which I do not venture to express my own opinion—that, in the "contraventions" and petty criminal cases disposed of by the Magistrates, the present registers of sentences may be dispensed with, substituting for them a book ruled in columns, in which should be recorded the particulars of each case, with only an entry of the prisoner's conviction or discharge, instead of an *in extenso* statement of the grounds on which the Magistrate has given his decision. These grounds being specified by the Magistrate in the presence of the accused, there would appear to be no reason why they should be preserved at length in the records of the Court. The cases are of a trivial nature, and I am informed that no one ever troubles himself to refer to them afterwards. The writing down of

42

The Inferior Courts.
the judgment by the Magistrate in each case can scarcely be supposed to exercise any moral restraint upon him in the discharge of his duty. Much time would be saved both to him and the Registrar under him if this change were made.

Registers of Deposits.
235. The registers of deposits into Court may be dispensed with in the Inferior, as is now the case in the Superior, Courts. With rare exceptions, not occurring more than once or twice a year in the Police Courts, as I am informed, deposits are accompanied by a schedule containing all the particulars relating thereto; and these particulars are copied into the registers, thus creating a duplicate, useless and cumbersome record. In the few instances in which no schedules are presented, the details of the deposits, now entered in the books, should be written on separate sheets, which would be equivalent to schedules, and such schedules and sheets should from time to time be bound in volumes and indexed. The withdrawal of a deposit should be noted on the schedule, instead of, as at present, being recorded in the register. In this manner more trustworthy and accessible records would be preserved and much unnecessary labour avoided.

Proposed Reductions in the Magistrates' Establishments.
236. Other alterations, tending to simplify the routine work of the Courts, would, I am convinced, suggest themselves to any unprejudiced person, better acquainted than I am with such matters, and more competent to suggest modifications conducive of economy without lessening the efficiency of the machinery for the administration of justice; but the reforms I have pointed out, if adopted, will, in my opinion, enable the City Magistrates' Courts to dispense with at least one of their three Registrars, and two of their five Assistant Registrars and Clerks. The two Marshals attached to the Civil branch of the Police Court in Valletta might also be dispensed with if writs and summonses were served by Policemen, as they now are in the Criminal branch and in the Syndics' Courts.

237. As the District Magistrates' Registrars are paid solely by fees, amounting to about £60 or £70 a year—of which, however, £40 is guaranteed by the Government—I do not recommend any change in their position. The reduction of the number of Syndics from seven to five will, of course, enable two District Registrars to be dispensed with, but a portion of their incomes would probably go in the shape of fees to enhance the emoluments of the others.

THE SUPERIOR COURTS.

The Superior Courts.
238. Besides the Vice-Admiralty Court, which now has little more than a nominal existence and entails no expense on the Government, the Judicial Establishments of Malta comprise a Criminal Court, a Civil Court, divided into First and Second Halls, a Commercial Court, and a Court of Appeal, the proceedings of which are conducted by a President, with a salary of £600 a year, and five other Judges, receiving £500 apiece. These stipends do not appear to me at all excessive, and, in deference to the strongly expressed opinion of nearly all branches of the legal community, I abstain from recommending any present reduction of their number, though I am not without hope that the changes I shall suggest, if enforced, will have so much effect, not only in simplifying the machinery for the administration of justice, but yet more in discouraging litigation, and thus greatly reducing the labours of the Judges, as to enable the island hereafter to dispense with the services of at least one.

239. In nearly all the suggestions I shall make, especially in those not strictly limited to the modification of clerical arrangements, I shall avail myself of the written opinions with which, after several interviews, I have been favoured by the President of the Court of Appeal, and which he has allowed me to print in the Appendix.[*]

The Criminal Court.
240. The duties of the Criminal Court are light, less than fifty cases, on an average, coming before it in the course of a year; and the only observations I have to offer concerning it refer to its system of registration and will be given presently.

---

[*] It may be well to quote the following letter:—
"Mio caro Sir Penrose.—In risposta al suo cortese biglietto in data di oggi, mi affretto di communicarle che io non ho alcun obbiezione perchè Ella faccia dei miei suggementi quell' uso che riputerà proprio. La prego di onorarmi dei suoi comandi e di credermi sempre pronto a potero contribuire, in quanto mi è possibile, pel compimento di quell' opera che in sin da tempo è da mi desiderata, pel bene del mio paese, e che io confido de vedere perfezionata per mezzo suo. Mi creda, mio caro Sir Penrose, suo sinceramente, Anto. Micallef. Misida, 24 Gen⁰, 1879." Of which the following is a translation:—"My dear Sir Penrose,—In reply to your kind note of this day's date, I hasten to state to you that I have no objection whatever to your making such use of my suggestions as you may think proper. I beg you to honour me with your commands, and to consider me always ready to contribute, as far as it is in my power, for the accomplishment of that work which I have long desired for the good of my country, and which I trust to see now accomplished through your agency. Believe me, my dear Sir Penrose, yours sincerely, Anto. Micallef. Misida, 24th January, 1879."

241. The Commercial Court is an adjunct of the Civil Court, the separate existence of which appears to be now quite unnecessary and inconvenient. Originally borrowed from Italian institutions, it was intended to be a Court in which experienced merchants, styled Consuls, were the principal authorities, a Judge being appointed only to aid them in their deliberations, and to see that their decisions were in harmony with the law. The Consuls, however, though still legally recognised and available when called upon, have long ceased to be employed, mainly perhaps because the commercial public has acquired sufficient and greater confidence in trained Judges, though it is noteworthy that their disappearance was coincident with a change in the law entitling them to claim fees for their services. One of the Judges, at any rate, now sits alone in the Commercial Court, and the business brought before him differs only in technical arrangements, for which the lawyers are responsible, from that brought before the Judges in the Civil Court; while confusion and delay frequently arise from uncertainty as to which of the two Courts should be appealed to by plaintiffs, and facilities are afforded for useless quibbles and prolonged litigation. Much additional expense is also attendant on the maintenance of a clerical staff for each Court. I therefore fully endorse Sir Antonio Micallef's recommendation that the Commercial Court be suppressed and its functions merged, by very simple alterations in the "Laws of Organisation and Civil Procedure," in those of the First Hall of the Civil Court.*

<small>THE SUPERIOR COURTS.</small>
<small>The Commercial Court.</small>
<small>Proposal to amalgamate it with the Civil Court.</small>
<small>* See Appendix C. (IV.).</small>

242. The First Hall of the Civil Court, which, if the suggestion in the next paragraph is adopted, would henceforth be styled merely the Civil Court, would probably require the occasional assistance of the Judge now occupied in the Criminal and Commercial Courts, in addition to the two who are exclusively engaged in its business; but some reduction of its work would result from the adoption of a suggestion made to me by one of those learned gentlemen to the effect that such cases, involving the examination of numerous witnesses—as those of affiliation, alimony, judicial separation, and breach of promise to marry—might properly be assigned to the Inferior or Magistrates' Courts, seeing that, as a rule, they deal only with matters of fact, and that, even when questions of law arise out of them, those questions are not of a difficult nature. There would be manifest convenience, moreover, in adopting the President's proposal, that " in cases of breach of promise a public act or a private writing should be the only admissible proof of the promise made, and not the evidence of witnesses."†

<small>The Civil Court, First Hall.</small>
<small>† See Appendix C. (III.).</small>

243. The Second Hall of the Civil Court is a tribunal of "voluntary jurisdiction," so called because its aid is invoked by persons desiring authority to engage in certain unopposed acts or proceedings, or sanction for certain acts to which, at the time of application, there are no opponents in the sense of litigants, as in the case of a married woman wishing to give security for her husband or to enter into a contract without her husband's consent, or in that of a guardian anxious to dispose of the property of a minor. This Court also appoints, confirms or removes, guardians; controls the disposition of property by imbecile, insane or prodigal persons; relieves heirs from certain liabilities connected with property accruing to them; legitimatises children not born in wedlock, &c. Important and various as its functions may be, the President is of opinion that they can, without inconvenience or prejudice to the public, be dealt with by the Judges sitting in the Court of Appeal, and that thus all the expenses incidental to the maintenance of a separate Court may be dispensed with.‡ I recommend that this suggestion be adopted, and that the Second Hall of the Civil Court, as an independent establishment, cease to exist.

<small>The Civil Court, Second Hall.</small>
<small>Proposal to amalgamate it with the Court of Appeal.</small>
<small>‡ See Appendix C. (V.).</small>

244. If that be done, and if also the proposal I have made as to the transference to the Superior Courts of appeals now made to the Magistrates' Civil Court of Second Instance § be followed, the three Judges, including the President, sitting together in the Court of Appeal proper as often and as long as may be requisite, will be able to employ some of their leisure in attending by turns both to appeals from the Magistrates' Courts and to cases of "voluntary jurisdiction," for which one Judge will be sufficient.

<small>The Court of Appeal.</small>
<small>§ See par. 224.</small>

245. The proposed reduction of the number of Superior Courts from five to three will greatly facilitate a complete revision of their clerical and semi-clerical establishments, and lead ultimately to a considerable reduction in the staff. If, moreover, as I have already suggested, the registration work now done in the Public Registry and the custody of some of the archives now held by it be transferred to the Courts, it will be possible to bring together all the duties of a kindred nature now performed by different branches of the service, and to place them in due subordination to the Judicial Bench, while at the same time rendering their relations with the public far more satisfactory than they now are.

<small>Proposed Economies in the Establishments of the Courts.</small>

246. At present the duties of the subordinate officers of the Court—ill-defined by law, if I may be allowed to say so—are very insufficiently performed.

THE SUPERIOR COURTS.
The Criminal Court Establishment.

247. The business of the Criminal Court is too simple for it to get much out of order. Sitting generally only one day a week, it appears to give very scanty occupation to the Registrar, with a salary of £170 a year, the Marshal at £85, and the Porter at £40, whom it is necessary to employ separately while the Court is a distinct establishment. The only suggestion I have to offer concerning them, therefore, is that their leisure time be utilised in other ways.

The Civil Courts Establishments.

248. In the various Civil Courts there is room for greater reforms. These four Courts, as at present constituted, employ three Registrars, each receiving £200 a year; one Registrar, who is also Archivist to the Courts, receiving £170; one Computist at £170; two Assistant-Registrars at £120 apiece and one at £110; thirteen Clerks, whose salaries amount to £990, while one of them is partly paid by fees, of which the total was about £66 in 1877, and several others receive fees of much smaller amounts; ten Copyists, paid by fees, which in 1877 amounted to £808; a Guardian at £40, and six Messengers receiving in all £200 a year. There is an Archivist of Notarial Acts, drawing a salary of £45 and such fees as he can collect; and in the Record branch of the Courts there are constantly employed, though not borne on the permanent establishment, a Keeper of Archives, four Clerks, two Bookbinders and one Fatigue man, for whom £480 are charged in the Estimates. In the more immediate service of the Judges there are also three Reporters or "Estensori delle Controversie," Advocates by profession, receiving respectively £45, £45 and fees amounting to about £25, and £75 a year; three Marshals at £85 apiece and one at £80; and five Porters at £40 each.

The Reporters or "Estensori delle Controversie."

249. The duties assigned by the "Laws of Organisation and Civil Procedure" to the Reporters are of a limited and apparently a redundant nature. They are chiefly to "take a note of the substance of the written pleadings of the parties and of the arguing of each case in Court, in order to be transferred in the register" (Art. 61). As that is a task more proper to the Registrar—or, as I shall propose, the Junior Clerk representing him—I am of opinion that, if these functionaries are retained, the suggestion of the President of the Court of Appeal should be adopted—that is, that they should be called upon, as occasion may require, to act as Supplementary Judges, as Election Commissioners, and as counsel for persons allowed to litigate *in forma pauperis*, as is now done in Gozo.*

* See Appendix C. (VIII. & IX.).

The Advocate for the Poor.

The retention of a separate officer as Advocate for the Poor, with a salary of £100 a year and a claim to pension, would then become unnecessary, and the occasional fees now paid for the other services referred to would either be saved to the public or go to make up the stipends of the Reporters. In any case those stipends call for readjustment, and, as their recipients are not debarred from the general exercise of their profession, should be looked upon merely as retaining fees, implying no claim either to permanent employment or to pension.

The Registrars.

250. The principal duties of the Registrars in the Civil Courts as prescribed by law are, (1) to register all the proceedings and orders of the Courts to which they are attached; (2) to transcribe, "or cause to be transcribed," the substance of the allegations of contending parties, as noted down by the Reporters; (3) to certify the authenticity of any copies that may be called for of acts or documents in their custody; (4) to keep such acts and documents without loss, mutilation or alteration for four years, and then to hand them over intact to the proper Archivist; and (5) to tax and assess judicial costs (Arts. 77 to 81). I find that the most important of those duties are almost entirely left to their Assistants and Clerks, while the Registrars themselves sit under the Judges in Court, performing trivial services, in the way of noting the progress of cases, &c., which could quite as well be carried out by junior Clerks. I propose that in future the duty of attending the Judges in Court be assigned to three Clerks, one each for the Court of Appeal, the Civil Court and the Criminal Court, who of course should be invested with the power of attesting witnesses, but whose time when not so occupied will be available for other clerical work. By this means the employment of five separate Registrars, as at present, will be rendered quite unnecessary.

Proposed Establishment of a General Registry.
† See par. 212.

251. If, as I have proposed, the whole registration work of the Courts together with that of the Public Registry † be concentrated in one establishment, the management of it should be assigned to one Chief Registrar, held responsible for the proper direction of the whole, assisted by three Assistant-Registrars, and ten Clerks, in addition to the three, a portion of whose time will be occupied in attending on the Judges in Court. It is impossible for me to estimate accurately the amount of labour that will be thrown upon each branch, and I do not contemplate its being divided by hard-and-fast lines; but I am of opinion that one Assistant-Registrar and two Clerks ought to suffice for the duties connected with the Court of Appeal and the Criminal Court; one Assistant-Registrar and four Clerks for those connected with the Civil Court, which will be more onerous

than the others; and one Assistant-Registrar and three Clerks for those connected with hypothecations, "insinuazioni," civil status acts, and the other business brought from the Public Registry; while the tenth Clerk, assisted by the Judges' Clerks, will probably be sufficiently occupied with so much as is retained of the work now done by the Computist and his Clerk.

The Superior Courts.

252. In order to relieve the General Registry from the labour and embarrassments which now oppress the offices of the several Registrars by their being made repositories of Court records and places of public search, I recommend the transfer to the Archives, at the end of each term, of all documents appertaining to all cases which shall have been closed for two terms.* They are now kept in the separate Registries for four years, and thus there is a constant accumulation of many hundred volumes and unbound parcels; and, as any one, on the smallest pretext, can claim the right of search without charge, this right is used to a much greater extent than it otherwise would be, and often, it is alleged, for the mere purpose of annoying the Department or particular employés in it. Thereby the records themselves are unnecessarily endangered, and the time of the Clerks is heavily taxed in complying with demands that might be more properly addressed to the custodians of the older records, who would, as they now do for other searches, exact a fee sufficient to cover, in part if not altogether, the cost of indexing and preserving them.

Proposed Transference of Court Records from the Registries to the Archives.
* See par. 264.

253. The services of the ten Copyists now employed in the Registries should be dispensed with, and parties to every suit should be required to furnish the necessary copies of original papers, as in other countries. I may here translate the remarks of the President of the Court of Appeal on this subject. "The office of Copyists," he says, "will become useless if parties, contemporaneously with the presentation of original papers, were also to present to the Registrar the copies of those papers required for the information of their opponents; such copies to be signed by the Advocate, to be certified as to their conformity with the original, and to be without blanks, abbreviations, corrections, erasures, or marginal additions, and written on good paper, with good ink, and in a clear hand. The Registrar should reject copies when not complying with the above regulations. All other copies of original papers already existing in the Registry, or of judicial proceedings issued by order of the Court, should be made by Clerks."† These Copyists are now paid by fees, which are at first received into the Treasury, and subsequently divided among them. They are generally, as vacancies occur, transferred to other branches of the public service as Clerks, but their service as Copyists is allowed to count for pension, and the Government is at the expense of providing them with office-room and stationery. The change I propose would extinguish all such liabilities. The present arrangement will probably have to continue until the Copyists now employed are absorbed into the clerical staff of the Government, unless some of them elect to quit the service and continue their calling as agents of the lawyers and the public; but no new ones should be appointed.

The Copyists.
† See Appendix O. (VII.).

254. Copying-presses will hardly be available for the business of the Courts, but, as regards such copying as remains to be done by the Clerks, considerable economy may be effected by the judicious use of printed forms, containing the elaborate phrases that are so plentiful and so often repeated in legal documents. Such documents ought in all cases to be duly charged for.

Savings in Clerical labour.

255. The system of doing gratuitously for the public what it ought to do for itself, which is a special affliction in Malta, should be systematically discouraged throughout this and all other branches of the public service.

Gratuitous Services to the Public.

256. Not only is much clerical work performed at the cost of the State which ought to devolve upon suitors, but so great is the indulgence shown to litigants, and such the laxity exhibited by the staff of the Law Courts and the expensive machinery of the Audit Department, that many hundreds of persons who have prosecuted their claims before the legal tribunals are allowed to depart without paying the small judicial costs for which they are liable. The consequence is, that sums amounting to £4921 17s. chiefly due before the end of 1860, having been written off as irrecoverable in 1863, further arrears from no fewer than 10,834 defaulters had accumulated by the end of 1877 to £4202 17s. 4d., which amount, after being investigated by a local committee, is also now considered to be in great part irrecoverable, and the bulk of which will doubtless also have to be as quietly and conveniently "written off." Not only is the Government thus deprived of its dues, but even the fees accruing to Copyists, with the collection of which the Department is charged, were in arrear at the same date to the extent of £122 12s. 9d., and it is to be considered whether the Government is not morally bound to make good to these employés the loss they have sustained through the defects of a system which they were powerless to remedy.

Unrecovered Judicial Costs.

The Superior Courts.

257. It is alleged that the cost of recovering these arrears by legal process would in many cases exceed the amount to be recovered, but such a plea furnishes no justification for the practice pursued, while the immunity which suitors have been permitted to enjoy is nothing short of an indirect encouragement to frivolous litigation. Among the 10,834 defaulters, I am told, are some of the most prosperous and influential merchants and traders in the island.

Remedy for the evil.
* See Appendix C. (VI.).

258. It appears to me—and I am strengthened in my opinion by the copious observations of Sir Antonio Micallef, to which I desire to call particular attention*—that a very simple and efficacious remedy for this monstrous evil may be found in requiring all judicial costs and Court fees, as far as they can be ascertained, to be paid in advance, or, when they cannot be so ascertained, in insisting either upon such a sum of money being deposited with the Registrar as he deems sufficient to cover them, subject of course to subsequent adjustment, or, at his discretion, upon approved security being given. The most frequent arrears have accrued in cases where the sum involved was less than twenty shillings, and, if the Registrar were held personally liable for all arrears below that amount, I believe that the loss to the revenue from these sources would in future be very small indeed.

Stamps for Court Fees.

259. I am of opinion, moreover, that the use of adhesive stamps for the payment of fees would, under careful organisation, be attended with advantage. If all documents on which fees are now chargeable were inadmissible before the Courts unless bearing the proper legal stamps, an effective check would be established between the sum due and the sums received. Stamps in sufficient quantities might from time to time be placed in the custody of the Registrar. Their nominal value should be debited to him in the books of the Receiver-General, and the sums paid weekly to that officer placed to his credit. The difference between the two amounts would be represented by the stamps remaining unused, and these should be verified from time to time by the Auditor-General.

260. In employing stamps for legal documents it would be convenient and economical to have as few values or denominations as possible, and with this view I suggest that a local committee be appointed to revise the tariff of Court fees appended to the "Laws of Organisation and Civil Procedure," with a view to their being made as uniform as is practicable in amount and, at the same time, to their application being extended to documents and services now furnished gratuitously, but which ought to be charged for. This recommendation applies not only to fees of Court, but also to those chargeable on the registration of hypothecations, civil status acts, &c., as well as to fees for searches and copies or extracts of documents in the Archives.

The Computist.

261. The gentleman now attached to the Courts with the title of Computist, having a Clerk to assist him, or to relieve him in case of absence, appears to be looked upon as a sort of auditor, documents upon which fees are to be claimed being sent to him to be taxed or checked. It is no part of his duty, however, to see that the fees are credited, or even asked for, and the independent existence of such a functionary, with a little establishment of his own, seems to serve rather as an excuse for neglecting the interests of the Government than an additional protection to the revenue. As the fees to be charged are all prescribed by law, any intelligent Clerk can assess them, and the duty is most likely to be well done if the Registrar is held directly responsible for its performance by one of his regular staff.

The Registrars of the Inferior Courts and the Assistant-Registrars.

262. The foregoing suggestions with reference to the establishment of the Chief Registrar to the Courts are applicable, *cæteris paribus*, to the Registrars of the Magistrates' Courts. The latter officers, being in direct relation with the Magistrates, must necessarily be separately responsible for the work assigned to them, and, as regards their financial duties, in direct relation with the Receiver-General and the Auditor-General. On account of these responsibilities, I am of opinion that the Registrars of the City Magistrates' Courts should receive an addition to their salaries of £30 apiece, and take senior rank to the Assistant-Registrars, but, like those Assistant-Registrars, draw the ordinary pay of Clerks in the Civil Service, according to the scheme to be hereafter detailed.† The Registrars of the District Courts, having only subordinate duties and not being regular members of the Civil Service, will of course hold a different position.

† See par. 294.

The Chief Registrar.

263. As the Chief Registrar will have important duties to perform, I consider that, ranking above Chief Clerks and on a level with the Heads of second class Departments, he should receive a salary of £350 a year, and, being responsible for the proper collection of Court fees, &c., give adequate security. He should also be a notary by profession, but be debarred, like all his subordinates, from private practice.

264. The principal changes that I consider necessary in the establishment charged with the custody of the Archives of the Courts are consequent on the suggestions I have already made, viz., that the records, now in the Public Registry, except those of historical and antiquarian interest, be transferred to this branch,* and also that the documents which it now receives after the lapse of four years from the Registrars of the several Courts be more promptly consigned to it.† The latter proposal will only increase the labours of the Archivist for the brief period during which he is disposing of the accumulations or arrears that will be suddenly handed to him, and for this brief period temporary assistance can be afforded by some of the employés who will be redundant in other Departments. To disencumber the office, and to make room for the records that will be transferred from the Public Registry, it will be necessary to remove certain documents to the Auberge d'Italie, in one story of which there is already a large collection under the charge of the Archivist of Notarial Acts, and of which the lower story can doubtless be obtained without difficulty by finding quarters elsewhere for the officer who at present occupies it. Additional room will be furnished, however, by the reduction of the Registrars' establishments; and the utilisation of much space now vacant or inappropriately occupied in the Court House itself is possible. The excellent classification of the Court Records by their present custodian will afford facilities for separating those which are old, and to which reference is seldom required, from those in more frequent demand both by the Courts and by the public. THE SUPERIOR COURTS.

The Court Archives and Notarial Acts.
* See par. 213.
† See par. 252.

265. With reference to the Notarial Acts preserved in the Auberge d'Italie, I observe that, although the law requires all such acts to be deposited, under certain penalties, with the Archivist within six months of their execution, and although commissioners or inspectors are appointed to see that the law is enforced, it is liable to be evaded. It appears that the Acts of one of the leading notaries of the island, lately deceased, have not been so deposited for the last fourteen years, and it is possible that serious consequences may result to many who are interested in these notarial instruments. Either the law should be enforced, or it should be repealed in order that people may not be misled by believing that deeds by which they hold valuable property are in the safe custody of the Government. The Custody of Notarial Acts.

266. The present Archivist of the Courts is also a Registrar, and all the duties for which he is responsible appear to be performed by a Keeper who is not on the fixed establishment. The subordinates of the latter functionary are in the same position. While deprecating any unnecessary increase of the number of permanent employés, who on retirement will have to be provided with pensions, I think that intelligent and competent individuals who are employed during the best years of their lives upon work which unfits them for subsequent occupation elsewhere ought not to be excluded from the rule which applies to other Civil Servants, and I recommend that the four Clerks in the Archives branch, if it is found desirable to retain their services, as well as the Keeper, be placed on a more permanent footing, with perhaps some slight increase to their wages, though without their being included in the regular clerical establishment. The Keeper of the Archives and his subordinates.

267. In any case it is desirable that the Archivist or keeper, while maintaining his subordinate relations with the Registrar, should be the actual custodian of the Archives, and that both he and the Archivist of Notarial Acts, in the Auberge d'Italie, should be under the control of the Chief Registrar. The Archivist to the Courts and the Archivist of Notarial Acts.

268. As Bookbinders are now constantly employed in the Archivist's establishment, and as it is expedient that they should continue to be so employed in order to prevent legal documents from passing out of the custody of the proper authorities, I recommend that the binding of manuscript volumes for all the Departments of the Government—each of which now seems to employ its own binder—be concentrated here, and that, if necessary, an additional binder be added to the two at present engaged. Considerable economy should result from such a change. Bookbinders.

269. I have not been able to make myself sufficiently acquainted with the necessities of the Courts and their dependencies, especially with a view to the effect of the proposed reforms, to feel justified in forming an exact opinion as to the number of Marshals, Porters, Messengers and other subordinate employés that will be hereafter required; but the present staff appears to me to be excessive, and I would urge that no future vacancies be filled up without careful consideration of the requirements of the service. Out of the seventeen men thus employed, I am inclined to think that at least seven, if not more, may be dispensed with. The Marshals, Porter, &c., of the Courts.

270. In the Court of Gozo, combining as it does certain judicial with its magisterial functions, somewhat anomalous arrangements necessarily result from the very laudable endeavour to economise the number of employés by assigning separate duties to the same individuals. The satisfactory amalgamation of the duties of the Court Registrar The Registrar and the Reporter in Gozo.

48

The Superior Courts.

and his Clerks with those that concern hypothecations, civil status acts, &c., furnishes a precedent for the similar arrangement that I have proposed for the establishments in Valletta. The combination of the functions of Reporter with those of Advocate for the Poor also shows that there can be no valid objection to the abolition of the latter office in the capital of Malta.

Hours of the Courts.

271. Reasonable representations have been made to me as to the inconveniences which arise from the practice of suspending the business of both the Superior and the Inferior Courts for an hour at midday in order that those engaged in them may take a midday meal. The Courts now open at 9 A.M., and business, if there is any to be done, continues till 3 P.M., with an hour's interval at noon. Not only is this arrangement out of keeping with the habits of the population, especially its poorer members who chiefly resort to the Courts in the early part of the day, often entailing upon them a serious and unnecessary loss of time; but, particularly during the hot months, it is generally distasteful to the Government servants and unprofitable to the Government, inasmuch as little or no work can be done in summer after dinner. I believe it would be beneficial and satisfactory to all concerned, if six consecutive hours were appointed for the business of the Courts, beginning at 7 A.M. in summer and 8 A.M. in winter.

The Crown Advocate.

272. I have thus far made no reference to the important office of Crown Advocate. The present occupant of that office is a gentleman of such rare ability and such well-earned eminence that it would be impertinent of me to speak of him individually. In his official capacity he is public prosecutor and is largely responsible for the conduct of prosecutions and for the due administration of justice in criminal cases; as counsel for the Government, he also has charge of all its civil suits; he is, moreover, its legal adviser on all other affairs, and, as such, prepares all its legislative regulations, and has a very large share in all legislative schemes presented to the Council of Government and submitted to Her Majesty's Secretary of State. To these duties and responsibilities others have been added in consequence of his intimate acquaintance with the conditions and requirements of the island, and he has become one of the principal advisers and agents of the Governor on all matters of public importance. Successive Governors and Her Majesty's representatives at home may congratulate themselves on commanding the services of so talented an auxiliary. When those services are no longer available, an occasion which it is to be hoped is very distant, it is to be expected that his successor's position will be more strictly in accordance with the rank and functions assigned to him by law, and in that case, I consider, the salary attached to the post may be reduced from £550 to £500 a year.

THE AUDIT OFFICE.

The Audit Office.

273. The Department responsible for the correctness of the accounts of the Government, and of which I treat last because it has to do with all the others, comprises an Auditor General, three Clerks, and a Messenger, at an estimated cost, including contingent expenses, of £974 a year. Owing, however, to the complete form in which the heads of the several Departments, acting as sub-accountants with the Treasury, render their accounts to that Department, which embodies them all in one statement for audit, the work done in the Audit Office is so limited in extent and of such a simple nature that in 1876 it was proposed by the Government, at the instigation of the Elected Members of Council, to assign it to the Chief Secretary, assisted by only one Clerk added to his establishment.

The desirability of maintaining it with increased Duties.

274. It is most desirable that an independent audit should be preserved, and, as there are no professional accountants or auditors to be found among the inhabitants of Malta, who could be called in periodically to examine the public accounts, after the plan adopted by railway, banking, and other large companies in England, I see no safe course open to the Government except that of maintaining a separate and distinct Audit Department. I am of opinion that such a course may be followed with advantage, and with avoidance of the present extravagant charges for seeing that the money voted by the local Legislature and sanctioned by the Crown is properly appropriated and accounted for, if the Department be called upon to perform other services which are not inconsistent with those of audit.

The making of Contracts and leases.
See par. 84.

275. The most important of those services I have already sketched out in some detail * I anticipate great benefit to the revenue, and improvement in the relations between the Government and the community, from the adoption of such arrangements as will relieve the disbursing and collecting Departments of all responsibilities connected with the

making of leases and contracts of all descriptions. The performance of those duties may, it appears to me, very properly, with the assistance of the Notary, devolve on the Audit Department, acting under the guidance of a Contract Committee. I propose, therefore, that the head of this Department be in future styled "Auditor-General and Director of Contracts," and, in addition to being a member of the Contract Committee, that he be held responsible for all details connected therewith, preparatory to the approval of tenders and the formal completion of the documents. THE AUDIT OFFICE.

276. Another service which I propose to assign to the Audit Department has to do with the preparation of the Annual and Supplementary Estimates. That service is now performed in the Chief Secretary's office, which, not being a finance branch, and having so many important administrative duties to fulfil, may fairly claim to be relieved from all the drudgery and details connected with the public accounts, while there would be great advantage in lightening the Chief Secretary's own responsibility as regards the finances of the island. The relief thus given to that officer would render it easier for him to carry out the duty more properly devolving upon him of, from time to time, personally inspecting the several Departments, for the sound administration of which, under the Governor, he is especially answerable. Occasional visits, for which he does not now find sufficient time, from an officer occupying the high position of the Chief Secretary, especially if made at unexpected intervals, would have a most salutary effect on the whole Civil Service. Preparation of the Estimates.

277. The Estimates, based on information obtained from the several Departments concerned, should, I consider, be laid before the Governor, and ultimately submitted to the Council, after consideration by and on the recommendation of an experienced body, instead of, as at present, being framed on the sole responsibility of any one individual. Such a body, to be called the Finance Committee, should, in my opinion, be composed of the Chief Secretary, as Chairman, and of at least three other members, the Auditor-General, the Receiver-General, and the Collector of Customs; and the duty of preparing the materials for its deliberations should, as in the somewhat parallel case of the Contract Committee, devolve on the Auditor-General. His office being the centre of financial records, he would be in a position to tabulate the proposed schemes, to explain their details to his colleagues on the Finance Committee, and, as a member of Council, to subsequently expound the several items to that body in laying the Estimates before it. Proposed Formation of a Finance Committee.

278. Under competent direction considerable improvements may be made in the arrangement of the Estimates. In one respect they are at present confused and misleading. Instead of showing, in one lump sum opposite to his name, what each employé receives from the public, it frequently happens that, if he is paid in various capacities, the items which go to make up his income are so scattered that the uninitiated find it difficult to discover what his entire official income really is. The same functionary appears, for instance, unnamed, in one part of the Estimates as a Chief Police Physician, and in another as Inspector of the Addolorata Cemetery, while his transport allowance is separately shown, and, to know what he receives as Chief Sanitary Officer, a Supplementary Estimate, the contents of which might just as well have been incorporated with the Annual Estimate, has to be consulted. Careful inquiry, moreover, is needed, to learn that the salaries of the Keeper of Court Archives and his staff of Clerks and Bookbinders, who, though not on the fixed establishment, have been regularly employed for many years, are provided for in an item under the head of "Administration of Justice (exclusive of Establishments)," intended "to continue the arranging of the Archives of the Courts of Justice, and the forming of an inventory of the books and papers existing therein." Such instances are plentiful. I believe that the Government would find less difficulty in obtaining the consent of the elected members of Council to its proposed expenditure if the Estimates were presented in a more simple and explicit form. Possible improvements in the Preparation of the Estimates.

279. In addition to the preparation of the Estimates, I consider that it should be the duty of the Auditor-General to make the calculations and reports necessary to determine the rates of pension to be assigned to Civil Servants on their retirement, to prepare quarterly returns of changes in the establishments, and to receive from the various branches requisitions for their ordinary monthly expenditure.* Calculations for Pensions, &c.
* See par. 30.

280. To the same Department should also be transferred from the Chief Secretary's Office the duty of collecting materials to be published in the *Government Gazette* and the Annual Blue-book, and the supervision of their printing.† The Government Gazette and the Blue-book.
† See par. 25

281. In the preparation of the Blue-book considerable economy might be effected by expunging from it a great deal of unnecessary information which is not only expensive to print, but the accumulation of which must involve much useless labour. Thus, in the Proposed Improvements in the Blue-Book.

THE AUDIT OFFICE.

earlier portion, after a long list of " Fees, duties, &c., levied on account of Government," a similar list is given of fees paid to Advocates, Surveyors, and others " not accounted for to Government." If the return of the earnings of Advocates, for instance, in Malta, were accurate, I am at a loss to know why they should be officially recorded; but I am assured on good authority that the return is altogether incorrect. When the information given is pertinent, moreover, it is often far more copious than it need be. In a very much spun-out list of all the employés in the Civil Establishments, for example, I find forty foolscap pages occupied with the names of all the Inspectors, Sergeants, and Constables in the Police Force. I am convinced that the Blue-book might, with advantage to every one but the redundant compositors employed in the Government Printing Office, be reduced to less than one-half of its present enormous size. If that were done, under proper management in the Audit Office, it would probably be a trustworthy publication; as it is, I find that, though this ponderous tome is sent home every year as an authentic source of information for the use of Her Majesty's Secretaries of State, the Chief Secretary is reported, in the official "Hansard," to have objected in the Council of Government on the 27th of March, 1878 (and his objection was substantially repeated two days later), to supply it to the Elected Members, on the ground that "many statistics which are to be found in it, on account of the very scanty information on this head within the reach of the Government, are not at all reliable."

282. The important additions which, as I suggest, should be made to the work of the Audit Office will not, in my opinion, necessitate any augmentation of its staff, especially as, in the most important of its new duties, it will be assisted by the Government Notary, whose business it will be to prepare, and furnish copies of, all contracts and leases entered into by the Director of Contracts.

283. It is, however, essential to the sound management of the financial affairs of the colony, not only that these new duties should be promptly and thoroughly performed, but that its present functions should be much better fulfilled than hitherto. It is incumbent on the Auditor-General to see, not only that the revenue and expenditure of the island are properly accounted for in the vouchers that come before him, but also that the Government is not defrauded of its rights by the failure of the sub-accountants in collecting the sums due to it. It is difficult to believe that, had proper attention been paid to this point, it would have been possible for the large arrears of rent for houses and lands, and of Court fees, together exceeding £12,000, to have been allowed to accumulate in the books of the Land Revenue Department and the Registries of the Superior Courts. It should be the business of this Department, not only to obtain returns showing that the sums received have been duly credited, but also to insist on prompt recovery of the sums outstanding.

284. If the duties of the Auditor-General, as I have sketched them out, are satisfactorily performed, his position will be second only to that of the Chief Secretary, and his Department will be of great service to the island. If things are to remain as they are, however, I must endorse the opinion expressed by the Elected Members of the Council and by the local Government itself, that the office may be abolished with advantage.

ESTABLISHMENTS.

ESTABLISHMENTS.

The Position of the Civil Servants in Malta.

285. The number of Government employés in Malta, even if reduced as I propose, is disproportionately large as compared with the establishments at home and in some other colonies. It must be remembered, however, that the climate of the island does not encourage either mental or bodily activity, and that as much energy cannot be looked for, either in Englishmen or in natives, as might be expected in cooler regions. Fortunately the cost of living is lower than in many other countries; and thus, by judicious arrangements, it is possible to neutralise any numerical excess by fixing the salaries at comparatively low rates. At the same time there can be no doubt that both food and house rent have been considerably and permanently raised in price since the decline of the exceptionally expensive period of the Crimean war; and that, though the domestic arrangements and habits of the Maltese are still happily much simpler than those of English residents among them, the contact of the two races, which might with advantage be brought into more intimate relations with one another than at present, almost forces on the native population certain expenses which formerly it was not called upon to incur. I consider, therefore, that no great saving ought to be looked for in the

amount annually spent in salaries, especially among the lower grades in the clerical establishments; whose members may fairly claim to divide among themselves nearly all the advantages that can be derived from diminution of their numbers. ESTABLISH-
MENTS.

286. There are at present, including two Acting Chiefs, twelve Heads of Departments in Malta. I have recommended that, when a successor is appointed to the present Chief Secretary to Government, the salary of £1300 a year be reduced by at least the £300 which is personal to the present occupant of the office. I do not think any change is necessary in the salaries of the Auditor-General, the Collector of Land Revenue, whom I propose henceforth to call the Receiver-General, or the Collector of Customs, each of whom now receives £500 a year; nor in those of the Superintendent of Ports, who draws £300 and fees; the Controller of Charitable Institutions, at £400; the Commissary of the Monte di Pietà, at £240; or the Librarian, at £200. I have proposed, however, that the salary of the Superintendent of Police be reduced from £500 to £400; that the offices of Cashier to the Treasury at £350, and of Superintendent of the Government Printing Office at £190 be abolished, and, that instead of a Registrar of Hypothecations at £80, with £200 additional as Notary to Government, and of five Registrars to the Superior Courts, with salaries amounting to £940, a Chief Registrar at £350 be employed. On the other hand, I have recommended the appointment of a Superintendent of Works at £300. The net saving that may thus be effected on the salaries of Heads of Departments, exclusive of the Court Registrars, who now rank with Chief Clerks; and of the Chief Land Surveyor, who will disappear, will therefore be ultimately not less than £570 a year.* The Heads of Depart-
ments; Pro-
posed
Economies.

* See Appen-
dix D. (I.).

287. The salaries of Her Majesty's Judges I do not propose to disturb. If, however, my recommendation that an establishment of three City Magistrates, with salaries rising from £200 to £350, and of seven District Magistrates, at salaries and allowances amounting to £177 each, be substituted for the present staff of five Magistrates of Judicial Police in Malta, rising from £200 to £240, with an addition of £70 to one, of three Magistrates in Gozo, rising from £180 to £200, and of seven Syndics at £177 each, the average saving will amount to about £800 a year. I consider, moreover, that on the appointment of a successor to the present Crown Advocate, his salary should be £500 instead of £550, and that on the removal of the present Advocate for the Poor, he need not be replaced, and the salary of £100 a year now attached to this office may be saved.† The Judges
and Magis-
trates ; Pro-
posed Econ-
omies.

† See Appen-
dix D. (II.).

288. In the various branches of the Civil Service, including the Registrars of the Courts, but exclusive of the Assistant to the Chief Secretary, who may fairly hold rank with the Heads of the less important Departments, and whose salary of £350 a year does not appear to me excessive, provision is made for ninety-five Clerks and employés known by other designations, though all of them performing clerical duties. Some of these gentlemen are reasonably dissatisfied with their salaries and prospects, and I consider that their position and the present somewhat arbitrary arrangements for their promotion may be greatly improved upon. The Clerks.

289. I think it well to quote the Chief Secretary's own account of these arrangements from a memorandum with which he has furnished me. "The present system of departmental promotion," he says, "was established by Her Majesty's Commissioners in 1837, and the only modification introduced in it was the one made by Sir Henry Storks, that the promotions should be departmental up to Clerk No. 1 only, and that the Chief Clerks should be appointed from the general service, according to seniority coupled with efficiency. This modification removed the inconvenience that a Clerk, happening to be in an office in which several vacancies occurred in a short time, should attain the position of Chief Clerk before other Clerks senior to him in the service who happened to remain behind, owing to the circumstance that few vacancies had taken place in the Department in which they were serving. By the present system, therefore, every Clerk may hope to rise by departmental promotion up to Clerk No. 1, but he is not to expect to be appointed Chief Clerk before others who are his seniors in the service should have attained that position; and on the other hand, a Clerk who has seen his juniors in other offices rise before him by departmental promotion will regain his position over them when he becomes a Chief Clerk, and thus will obtain much more in one step than they obtained in several steps. According to the present distribution of salaries, there is besides departmental promotion, another chance of being promoted, that is to say, by being transferred to other Departments where the junior situations have comparatively good salaries attached to them and are always occupied by senior Clerks, the duties to be performed being of some importance and requiring therefore, together with efficiency, a practice in official matters which is only acquired after some years' service. By these transfers a Clerk at £90, for instance, in a certain Department is appointed to the last The Present
System of
Promotion.

ESTABLISH-
MENTS.

situation in the Treasury or the Audit Office, with a salary of £100 a year, and a Clerk of £100 or £110 is appointed to the last situation in the Chief Secretary's Office, with an annual salary of £120. Thus all the Clerks, in whatever office they may happen to serve, are made to partake of the advantage of a general Civil Service, without losing the benefits of departmental promotion. This system has always worked admirably well, both in the interest of the public and of the civil servants." My observations do not enable me to endorse that opinion. The scheme appears to me to be objectionable in itself, and it is not invariably followed.

Its Defects; Injustice to the Clerks:

290. There is neither complete fusion nor entire separation between the Civil Establishment, strictly so called, and the Registries of the Courts or the Public Registry. With few exceptions, the clerical arrangements in all alike are so much akin that the duties of the Clerks might be interchangeable, and it sometimes happens that changes not always advantageous are made; but at other times Clerks are debarred from the advancement they have a right to expect on the ground, not only that the Judicial Establishments are distinct from the Civil Establishments, but even that, in separate branches of those establishments, promotion ought to be local. When this rule is adhered to, moreover, it sometimes leads to unsatisfactory results. Very few of the Departments in Malta include more than five or six Clerks. In some there are only three or four. As the rule, subject to important exceptions, is that a Chief Clerk shall receive £180 a year, with £60 additional after being thirty years in the service, a Clerk No. 1 £120, a Clerk No. 2 £100, a Clerk No. 3 £90, a Clerk No. 4 £80, a Clerk No. 5 £75, and a Clerk No. 6 £70, chance or favour can have an important effect in determining the prospects of different Clerks for promotion. Out of five Clerks who entered the service in 1857, for instance, I find that the senior is a Clerk No. 1, receiving £130 a year, the next is a Clerk No. 3 at £130, the third a Clerk No. 1 at £120, the fourth a Clerk No. 1 at £150, and the fifth a Clerk No. 2 at £140. Out of four admitted in 1863, again, the first is a Clerk No. 3 at £75, the second a Clerk No. 3 at £90, the third a Clerk No. 2 at £110, and the fourth a Clerk No. 1 at £120, with special allowances amounting to £30. As the last indicated is a Clerk No. 1, he is supposed to have prior claims to a Chief Clerkship over ten seniors who happen to be Clerks No. 2 or 3, while he already draws a higher pay than any of seven out of the eight Clerks No. 1 who are senior to him. I have nothing to say against this particular gentleman, who doubtless fully earns the salary he receives and is one of the most promising men in the service, but his merits do not lessen the just grievances of the men who have been practically to a great extent superseded by him. If I refrain from quoting other instances as striking, it is not because they are not forthcoming.

Inconvenience to the Government.

291. Another evil consequence of the existing arrangements, affecting the Government rather than its employés, is that Clerks who have been kept for many years, perhaps nearly a quarter of a century, in one Department, and who are therefore, if fit for anything, specially competent to continue working in it with advantage, have a right to expect, after serving for a reasonable time in the rank of Clerk No. 1, to be promoted to a Chief Clerkship, though under present arrangements such a Chief Clerkship, when vacant, is almost certain to be in some other Department, about the duties of which they know nothing, and for the management of which they cannot be expected to show any particular aptitude. I have before me the case of a gentleman, of whom again I desire to say nothing at all disparaging, who, on the occasion of a new Chief Clerk having to be appointed, was, without any special qualifications to fit him for the office, transferred from another Department to fill the post instead of the experienced Clerk No. 1 already there.

The new arrangement proposed.

292. In such an island as Malta, where each Department has only a small staff of employés, it appears to me that the only equitable and expedient arrangement is to constitute one general establishment of Clerks, all of whom, if they display an average amount of intelligence and industry, shall have a right to advance towards the highest emoluments that the Government can afford to pay them, and who may look forward to ultimately earning, by special industry and intelligence, promotion to the superior position held by Heads of Departments. I earnestly recommend that such an establishment be constituted without delay, and, in my opinion, the numerical reductions I have proposed will justify some slight and gradual augmentation of the salaries paid to nearly all but the youngest members of the service. There are in this island, perhaps in larger proportion than in other colonies, some elderly Civil Servants who, from their ignorance of the English language, or from other defects, are comparatively useless, and who, if they are allowed to retain their present positions until the time comes for them to retire, can hardly feel aggrieved at being passed over by younger and abler men, and I think that the salaries paid to novices in their teens, if small in

themselves, are out of proportion to the salaries they can hope to attain, and will be in urgent need of to meet the growing demands of their domestic surroundings, after they have been ten, fifteen, or twenty years in the service. I do not propose, therefore, to increase the stipends of either of these two classes. But I trust that the scheme I shall put forward will be found to be equitable in itself, tolerably satisfactory to the members of the Civil Service in Malta, and conducive to the proper execution of the business assigned to it.

Establish-
ments.

293. I have recommended that the clerical strength of the Chief Secretary's Office be reduced by one, that of the Customs Department by one, and that of the Police Office by two; that, on the Treasury being merged with the Land Revenue Department in the Receiver-General's Office, only one member of its present staff be retained; that, on the amalgamation of the Public Registry and the Registration branches of the several Superior Courts, the present number of Registrars, Assistant-Registrars, and Clerks be reduced by thirteen; and that three Clerks be also dispensed with in the establishments of the Magistrates' Courts. There will thus be a reduction of twenty-three from the total of ninety-five Clerks now provided for in the Estimates. Out of those ninety-five ten are Copyists, who, as I have suggested, ought not to form part of the Civil Service, and who should disappear from it as soon as the present men are absorbed or withdrawn. At present, I understand there are only eight Copyists to whom the Government is pledged to give permanent employment; and one of the regular Clerks, having only received a temporary appointment during my visit to the island, need not be at present confirmed. If the now vacant offices of Collector of Land Revenue, or Receiver-General, and of Controller of Charitable Institutions are filled up by promotions from the clerical establishment, the entire force of that establishment will be reduced to ninety, of whom eight, as Copyists, will be paid by the fees received from the public for the work done by them, though for some time to come they will swell the number of supernumeraries in the reformed Civil Service. After taking account of the present or immediately probable vacancies, it will be seen that there are as many as twenty-seven such supernumeraries to be disposed of, before the present estimated establishment of ninety-five can be curtailed to the strength of sixty-three, which is all I consider necessary. As several gentlemen in the service are far advanced in life, and cannot be expected to do much more efficient work, it may be assumed that this number will be quickly reduced. Moreover, though I am of opinion that the present arrangements as regards Copyists are objectionable, and ought to be altered as soon as is convenient, they may be prolonged, in a modified form, so as to utilise the services of some of the supernumeraries, who, while drawing the salaries now assigned to them as Clerks, will enable the Government to partly recoup itself by crediting the fees paid for their work as Copyists. In this way the redundant list of twenty-seven may be at once brought down to seventeen, by detaching from it not only the eight Copyists, but also, if so many as ten are necessary, two Clerks to be associated with them.

Reductions in the Clerical Staff.

294. In order to improve the position and prospects of the sixty-three gentlemen who will form the future fixed clerical establishment, I propose that—all distinctive titles such as Chief Clerk, Clerk No. 1, Clerk No. 2, Computist &c., being abolished, and such other titles as Registrar, Assistant-Registrar, &c. being retained only for convenience of reference without constituting any barrier between their holders and other Clerks—the whole body be divided into the following sections:—three Probationary Clerks, who, while so employed, shall not have any claim to permanent employment, but who, if confirmed, shall be allowed to count their probationary service for pension, and whose salaries, starting at £50 a year, shall rise by annual increments of £5 to £60; fifteen Fourth Class Clerks, beginning at £60 and rising by annual increments of £4 to £80; fifteen Third Class Clerks, rising by annual increments of £5, from £90 to £120; fifteen Second Class Clerks, rising by annual increments of £5 from £130 to £180; and fifteen First Class Clerks, rising by annual increments of £10 from £190 to £250. The addition of £60 a year now made to the salaries of Chief Clerks after thirty years' service should be discontinued, and the only variation from the regular scale should be in the special allowance of £30 a year, made, as I have already suggested,* to the Registrars in the City Magistrates' Courts, whether they are First, Second, or Third Class Clerks, on account of the responsibilities of their office.†

Proposed Amalgamation of the whole Clerical Staff and Improved scale of Salaries.

* See par. 262.

295. Whenever a vacancy occurs, promotion from each rank to the rank above it should go by seniority, provided the Head of the Department in which the gentleman having a claim to promotion is serving satisfies the Governor that he is in all respects worthy of advancement. It is desirable that great care should be taken to see that none but suitable men are promoted, and the rigour of selection should be increased for each higher grade in the service; but it should be clearly understood that every employé has

† See Appendix D. (III.). Proposed Rule as regards Promotion.

Establishments.

a right to be advanced in his turn, if he shows satisfactory diligence and ability. At the same time, especially in the selection of Heads of Departments, the authorities should not only feel themselves at liberty, but should make it their duty, to choose for each post the fittest man that can be found, in whatever grade or branch of the service he may be.

Probable Advantages of the Proposed Scheme.

296. By the proposed scheme it will be possible, without injury to individuals, for Clerks either to remain for a very long period, even the whole of their official career, in one Department, or to be frequently removed from one to another, the convenience and advantage of the Government being the only object to be sought. There can be no reason against several senior Clerks being at the same time in one Department, or hardly any but juniors in another, if by such an arrangement the public interests are served.

297. By the arrangement of classes and gradual increase of salary which I have proposed, I believe that no Clerk now in the service will be in any way injured, and that nearly all will be greatly benefited. The proposed scheme, while giving to all a fair prospect of higher salary after long service than is now generally obtained, will, I apprehend, secure most advantage to those who, after fifteen or twenty years' service, usually with large families to provide for, now find their position too often a very hard one.

Economies to be expected from it.

298. As I have, of course, been unable to form any safe opinions as to the relative merits of all the Clerks, of whom a portion will have to be regarded as supernumeraries, while the others will have to be grouped in the several classes, questions which must necessarily affect the precise economical bearings of the scheme, I refrain from printing the calculations which I have made. Those calculations, however, appear to show that the plan I have suggested, if adopted at once and burdened with the cost of all the supernumeraries to be provided for, would not add more than £250 to the amount, £9370, now allowed for the salaries of all the members of the service who would be included in its operations. I do not propose, however, that the scheme should be completely enforced until the supernumeraries have been absorbed, and as the ultimate cost of the new establishment will vary between a minimum of £7260 and a maximum of £9690, the ultimate economy may, I think, be estimated at an average of about £800 or £900 a-year.

Subordinate and Professional Members of the Civil Service.

299. In this proposal I have taken no account either of the very large numbers of subordinate members of the Civil Service, including Messengers and others in the public offices, as well as Policemen and employés in the Charitable Institutions, the Customs, and elsewhere, or of the professional men of various grades and callings, who in Malta are considered to belong to the Civil Service, and to be entitled to pensions on retirement from it. Among these professional men are the Reporters, Interpreters, and others attached to the Courts, and the much more numerous body of Physicians and Surgeons employed in the medical service of the Government. As regards all these employés, I need add little to what I have already said in previous portions of this Report. I hope that experience will prove the practicability and wisdom of greater reductions in numbers and expense than I have felt myself competent, after such examination as I have been able to make as a lay visitor, to definitely propose.*

*See Appendix D. (IV.)

Professional Auxiliaries.

300. One point, however, I have no hesitation in insisting upon. Resident Physicians, Apothecaries, and others in hospitals and elsewhere, like legal employés in the Courts, may very properly become regular servants of the Government, and in that case should not only be paid adequately for the duties they have to perform, but also have a prospect of superannuation after their term of useful labour is exhausted. But all, whether doctors, lawyers, or others, who are not in the exclusive service of the Government, and who look to outside exercise of their professions for a part of their income, small or large, should be paid only for such work as they actually do, without being allowed to claim on account of it any prospective reward in the shape either of permanent employment or of ultimate pension. Out of the £10,269 17s. 9d. now paid to two hundred and eighty-five pensioners, a large part ought never to have been incurred, and the liabilities with which the Government has improperly saddled itself will, I have no doubt, be considerably greater than they now are, when its professional auxiliaries are of an age to claim retirement. This error should be carefully avoided in future.

301. The same remark applies to such other professional agents of the Government as the Periti or Surveyors now connected with the Land Revenue and Public Works Department. Whether these Periti should be paid simply by fees for the work they actually do, or should be included in the regular Civil Service, I leave to be hereafter decided; but henceforth no permanent appointments should be given to persons who claim the right of increasing their incomes by private practice. At the same time, seeing that there appear to be several Clerks who, as bookkeepers and even notaries,

and in other capacities, find it possible to earn something by working for private employers out of their office hours, I think no objection should be made to their doing so, provided the Heads of their Departments do not consider that their office hours or their official duties are thereby interfered with. *Establishments.*

302. There are, of course, several classes of subordinate employés—such as the Marshals and Porters in the Courts; the Storekeepers, Gaugers, Overseers and Guardians in the Customs; the Warders, Nurses, and other servants in the Hospitals, Asylums, and Prisons; the Keepers of Lighthouses, and the Boatmen employed by the Superintendent of Ports; the members of the Police Force, and the Messengers and others in the various Departments—many of whom, being permanent servants of the Government, are entitled to regular wages and the prospect of pensions. After what I have already said concerning some of them, it is only necessary now for me to express my opinion that in certain branches of the service their numbers will bear considerable reduction, though to what precise extent I am not in a position to decide, and that the work assigned to some of them might be more cheaply and satisfactorily done by persons engaged simply by the day, week, month, or other brief and clearly defined period. In Malta, even more than in many other colonies, there is a constant effort to fasten upon the Government the responsibility of providing for crowds of dependants, who are often no better than pensioners long before they are formally superannuated; but it is almost idle to protest against this communistic tendency unless the Government is itself firm and prudent enough to resist it. *Subordinate Employés.*

303. Regarding the Civil Service generally I have one or two other suggestions to offer.

304. I find that great laxity prevails as to the appropriation of the transport or travelling allowance sanctioned in the case of certain employés whose duties require, or are supposed to require, their visiting places distant from their regular offices. This allowance appears to be generally accepted as an irregular addition to the salary of the individual enjoying it, and to imply no sort of obligation to spend it in the public service, either by making such journeys as ought to be made in the interests of the Government, or by making them in such ways as will conduce to most economy of official time. In addition to £737 voted under the head of transport for the current year, and exclusive of the allowances to the Syndics for travelling and other expenses, as much as £405 is charged in the Annual Estimates for transport allowances, varying from £30 to £50 apiece, to certain officers. I propose that all these allowances be at once discontinued, and that an arrangement be entered into by the Director of Contracts with one or more private individuals for the supply of such carriage, horse, or boat conveyance as may be required from day to day by these or any other employés on behalf of the Government. If the requisitions for such occasional transport were confirmed by the Heads of the several Departments concerned, and the service, when rendered, were duly vouched and charged under the head of transport, I am convinced that great economy would be effected, and at the same time the duties for which travelling is necessary would be much more frequently and thoroughly performed than at present. *Travelling Allowances.*

305. I have already suggested that the hours of business in the Law Courts should be altered. As the natives of Malta are accustomed to rise early and to make their principal meal in the middle of the day, after which, especially in summer, some time for repose is necessary, a much better day's work could be generally obtained from the Government employés if they began it earlier. Some of the offices now open at eight o'clock, some at nine, and all have a break of an hour or more, at twelve or one o'clock, before closing at three or four. If in most of the offices the hour for commencing were fixed at seven in summer and eight in winter, it would not be unreasonable to expect attendance in the Government offices, without interruption, for six consecutive hours. In this way at least an hour's time, and considerably more than an hour's work might be gained by the Government, with convenience and comfort, as I am assured by some of the most industrious of them, to the Clerks themselves. *Office Hours.*

306. As soon as the Civil Service of Malta has been reformed, and its professional assistants as well as its Heads of Departments and regular Clerks can be enumerated, it would be desirable that it should be specified in a new Civil List—not to be augmented without the sanction of Her Majesty's Secretary of State—which as a whole could be every year laid before the Council of Government, without the recognised Civil List being supplemented as at present by a tedious and confusing series of charges to be separately voted. *Proposed Revision of the Civil List.*

THE ENGLISH LANGUAGE IN MALTA.

The English Language in Malta.

Its Previous Neglect.

307. In earlier pages of this Report I have frequently had to touch upon a question of great importance, and one to which, in Mr. Herbert's letter, I was requested to pay special attention; viz. "how far it will be desirable to promote the use of English as the official language of the colony."

308. On every ground it is to be regretted that throughout the period of nearly eighty years during which Malta has been a British dependency, so little effort has generally been made in this direction. It is neither to be expected nor desired that the Maltese language should be eradicated, and any attempts to interfere with its colloquial use would certainly be injudicious and productive of nothing but dissatisfaction among the people to whom it is endeared, and to the expression of whose thoughts in familiar conversation it is well adapted; nor, I need hardly say, do I suggest that the use of Italian, which is now common among the more educated classes, should be in any way forcibly restrained. The persistent encouragement which, until recent times, and in some respects to the present day, has been given to Italian in preference to English as the official language of the island and an auxiliary to the vernacular is, however, not more strange as an exhibition of mistaken tolerance than deplorable in its effects on the condition and prospects of the people of the island. By this means political agitators have been assisted in gaining a few converts to their theory that the Maltese, though really of alien race and temperament, are akin to the Italians, and ought to look forward to a union with the kingdom of Italy instead of that of Great Britain, and greater mischief has resulted from the perpetuation of prejudices that have seriously lessened the opportunities of progress which were brought within reach of the people by their connection with the British Empire.

Its Importance to the Population.

309. The dense and rapidly growing population of the island finds no adequate outlet for its energy among the Italian-speaking communities, and, by its prevailing ignorance of the language, is almost debarred from participation in the advantages offered to emigrants resorting to English-speaking countries. The frugality and industry shown by the Maltese generally—especially by those most separated from the contaminating influences of town-life, among stragglers and adventurers from all the ports of the Mediterranean, and with so large an admixture of soldiers and sailors as is to be found in Valletta and its suburbs—are most remarkable and most praiseworthy; but it is evident that the agricultural resources of Malta and the neighbouring island of Gozo, having a total area of but 115 square miles, including much barren rock, are already immensely overtaxed for the support of their population, which, exclusive of the British troops, had risen from 115,570 in 1837 to 134,055 in 1861, and to 151,082 in 1877; while the manufacturing and commercial opportunities of the colony, deteriorated in recent years, and constantly threatened by the vicissitudes of trade and the greater prosperity of other localities, are even now by no means adequate to the necessities of the people. The painful struggle for existence to which so large a proportion of the inhabitants is condemned, the alarming increase of pauperism, and the yet more alarming extent of infant mortality, attest the redundancy of the population, for which the only corrective appears to be a large and steady flow of emigration. A great obstacle to emigration, however, offers itself in the strong family feeling and insular prejudice which is fomented by the lack of sympathy with English institutions and habits, and which a knowledge of the English language would go far to remove, while that knowledge would of course be of the utmost advantage in enabling young persons, who can look forward to little better than starvation at home, to improve their own condition and be of service to those they leave behind them by seeking better fields of enterprise in more sparsely-peopled countries, and especially in other British colonies. That is a very brief statement of the general grounds for my conviction that everything it is possible and legitimate for the Government to do should be done by it towards encouraging the whole population of Malta to make itself acquainted, at any rate in a rudimentary way, with the English language.

Former Efforts to Encourage it.

310. The importance of this step in the interests of the whole community, and the most proper ways in which it could be aided by the Government, were recognised so far back as 1820 by Sir Thomas Maitland, the first Governor of the colony, as appears from the following Minute dated the 17th of May of that year;—" With a view to encourage a more general study of the English language among the natives of this island, his Honour the Lieutenant-Governor, with the previous approbation of His Excellency the Governor, has been pleased to order and direct as follows:—1. That no person shall henceforth be admitted to act as an advocate, notary, or law procurator in Malta unless he can read, write and speak the English language. 2. That all petitions addressed to Government, excepting

those for appeals to the Supreme Council of Justice, shall be written in English. From this rule, however, will be excepted, for the present, the petitions from individuals of the lower classes in the different casals in the country, which will continue to be received in Italian until the end of the present year, after which those petitions also must be written in English. 3. That after the 1st of January, 1821, all contracts with Government will be made out in English and the parties must provide themselves, if they require it, with an Italian copy. 4. That in filling up any vacancy which may henceforth occur in the Civil Establishment of this island, or in making any new appointment, a preference will always be given to those among the natives who may be acquainted with the English language." The first and fourth articles of that Minute were confirmed by another, written by Governor the Hon. F. C. Ponsonby, on October 1st, 1827; but most unfortunately the wise beginning thus made towards establishing the English language in Malta was not adhered to or improved upon. THE ENGLISH LANGUAGE IN MALTA.

311. I express not only my own opinion but also that of intelligent representatives of nearly every section of the community with whom I have discussed the subject, in saying that a great error was committed by the late Sir George Cornewall Lewis and Mr. John Austin, the special commissioners who visited this island in 1837, and did so much to improve its institutions, when they recommended that preference should be given to Italian over English in the educational and other establishments of the colony, on the plea that, "from its use as the language of trade throughout the Mediterranean and from the near neighbourhood of Malta to Italy and Sicily, the Italian language is far more useful to a Maltese than any other language, excepting his native tongue." Experience has not justified that assumption. The trade of Malta with the Italian kingdom amounted in 1877 to less than 2 per cent. of its trade with all the rest of the world, while its commercial relations with Egypt were of more than thrice the value, and those with Turkey nearly eleven times as great. In spite of all that has been done to encourage the use of Italian in Malta, moreover, it appears that when the Census of 1861 was taken only about one person in nine professed to speak the language and only one in ten to be able to write it, notwithstanding the very limited acquaintance which was allowed to pass as knowledge. The patronage which most of the English rulers of Malta have bestowed upon the Italian language to the detriment of their own has, therefore, not been very successful. It has, however, perpetuated the system of the foreign Knights who oppressed the island during nearly four centuries, in making Italian, which was in their time the language of the Church and of *belles lettres* in southern Europe, the language also of commerce, of the learned professions and of refined society. With the great aptitude for acquiring languages which the Maltese appear generally to possess, there can be no reason why the educated classes should not continue to be as familiar with Italian in addition to their native tongue as they now are; but the English Government owes it to them as well as to itself to promote among the people, by all fair means, a knowledge of the only language that can really help them in their laudable rivalry with the inhabitants of other countries and of all other British possessions. Subsequent Preference for Italian.

312. The most direct action towards this end which it appears to me incumbent on the Government to take is to insist on all its employés being thoroughly acquainted with English, and using it constantly, to the exclusion as far as possible of all other languages, in their official relations with the public. A great improvement has undoubtedly taken place in this respect during recent years, partly on account of the more stringent requirements imposed upon all candidates for admission into the Civil Service by competitive examinations. As clerkships are much sought after by young men in Malta, there being a great number of candidates for every vacancy, the general effect of the rule making obligatory a sufficient knowledge of the English language cannot fail to be considerable, and I am glad to record my satisfaction not only with the linguistic proficiency but also with the general intelligence of nearly all the junior Clerks who have entered the service during the past few years. If this rule is strictly adhered to, its effects will be very beneficial, though I consider that they might be further enhanced by abandoning the present practice of allowing candidates to obtain as many marks for knowledge of Italian as for knowledge of English, seeing that thus the candidate showing the highest proficiency in the only language that is important to him in his official capacity would have greater prospect of success in competition with others whose mastery of Italian literature, however commendable in its way, is useful chiefly as a social ornament. The rule insisting upon all Civil Service Clerks having a knowledge of English does not, however, apply to subordinate employés. As regards all such persons, it should, I consider, be insisted on with certain modifications. In the case of many, especially policemen, weighers and measurers in the Custom House, servants in the Charitable Institutions, warders in the Corradino Prison, and so forth, Proposed Insistance on the use of English as the Official Language in the Civil Service;

THE ENGLISH LANGUAGE IN MALTA.

other qualifications may be of greater importance than a colloquial acquaintance with English, but, from the first, I think that due account should be taken of such acquaintance in making new appointments and in regulating the scales of pay and prospects of promotion. In the case of all these subordinates much must depend on the discretion and energy of the Heads of Departments who have to deal with them. The same remark applies to the relations of both clerks and subordinates with those classes of the people who, as a rule, speak no language but the Maltese. A long time must necessarily elapse before it will be to the interests either of the public service or of the lower classes of the population for the native language to be excluded from official communications, but there is no reason why Italian should be recognised. The habit which prevails in many offices of conversing not only in Maltese but in Italian is much to be deprecated, and yet more objectionable is the practice of keeping books and preparing documents for record or transmission to the public in Italian. By these means many clerks who appear at one time to have been tolerably proficient in English have been encouraged to forget nearly all they knew. It should, at any rate, be insisted upon that all books and documents in every branch of the service be kept solely in English; that no account for payment or any other claim upon the Government be accepted unless prepared in that language; that, except in rare and unavoidable instances, no communications with the public be made in Italian; and that no clerk be eligible for promotion from his present rank, and especially no Head of a Department be appointed, unless he has acquired and retained a thorough knowledge of English.

In the Government Schools;

313. As regards the general spread of education it is not within my province to speak at any length, especially as Mr. Keenan has lately been commissioned to report on this subject. I may be allowed, however, to urge that, until far greater pains are taken than at present to give instruction in English, not only in the primary and secondary schools, but even in the Lyceums and the University, it cannot be expected that boys and young men there instructed will, without exceptional effort on their part, acquire any adequate knowledge of the language. I am told that even the examination in this respect of students intending to become advocates, and to enter other professions for which it is prescribed that they should be "conversant in the English language," is generally only an idle ceremony, the examiners in English being themselves almost entirely ignorant of the language, and sometimes performing their duties in so lax a manner that if, at an examination, one student is able to make a passable version of the few Italian sentences appointed for translation, his manuscript can be handed round for all the others to copy from it. If this state of things cannot be speedily improved upon, it is at any rate incumbent on the Government to insist that every professional man who enters its service, whether in a judicial or magisterial capacity, as a physician or as a chaplain, shall supplement his University diploma by trustworthy evidence that he is really and not only nominally acquainted with the English language. If in the learned professions there is at present such an utter dearth of English-speaking students, that any vacancies which may speedily arise could not be satisfactorily filled if the proposed rule were adopted, it might be advisable to fix its enforcement at a period two or three years distant, so as to afford time for aspirants to official employment to complete their education in this very important particular.

and especially the Orphan Asylum;

314. Without touching on the general question of education, I may here call attention to what appears to me to be a grave defect in an educational establishment which, being included among the Charitable Institutions, is more especially under the immediate control of the Government. In the Orphan Asylum in Valletta, Italian is the only language taught in addition to the mother tongue of the inmates. As these inmates are retained here for several years at considerable expense to the public, with the express object of training them to be useful members of the community and generally to be fitted for employment in trades or domestic service, it is very desirable that their education should be as helpful to them as possible, and there can be no doubt that instruction in English would greatly enhance their prospects of advancement in the future. Such instruction could be imparted to them almost without labour or expense if the attendants upon them were themselves acquainted with English, and in the habit of conversing with them in that language. This suggestion applies also to the small Foundling Hospital now at Floriana, from which most of the children are transferred when they are old enough to the Orphan Asylum, and which I have proposed to place under the same roof.

in the Council of Government;

315. One difficulty caused by the neglect of the English language in Malta has already been so far overcome that its entire removal ought now to be easy. Great confusion and frequent embarrassment formerly resulted from the strange custom of allowing members of the Council of Government to address the Governor and their colleagues

in either Italian or English, and even a few years ago much temporary inconvenience might have followed from prohibiting the use of Italian by the several members, both official and elected, who were ignorant of English. Now, however, there remains only one member who is not quite competent to speak in that tongue, and I am confirmed even by the expressed opinions of the principal elected members in the belief that no real injury to individuals, while at the same time great advantage to the community, would result from the passing of a short ordinance constituting English the only language in which the proceedings of Council may be conducted or officially recorded. As an indirect, but not insignificant, consequence of such an ordinance the colony would be spared the expense of issuing estimates and statements of revenue and expenditure, draft Ordinances and the texts of those that are passed by Council, and many other documents, in Italian as well as in English, and much costly labour in translating from one language to another would thus be avoided. It is also worthy of consideration whether the qualification for the political franchise, which is identical with that for jurorship as laid down in Article 517 of the Criminal Code of 1854, and which requires the juror to be "competently versed in the Italian language," should not, at no distant date, be so altered as to substitute English for Italian, or at any rate to give as much value to the former as to the latter language. THE ENGLISH LANGUAGE IN MALTA.

316. Another difficulty cannot, I fear, be so readily got rid of, though its removal appears to me almost more important than anything else that can be done towards encouraging the English language in Malta and enabling the Maltese to take their proper place as British subjects. The unfortunate arrangement by which Italian is the only language authorised to be used in the pleadings and judgments of the Law Courts has undoubtedly had a most prejudicial effect on the whole community. Not only has a numerous body of judges, magistrates, syndics, advocates, procurators, notaries and others been trained up far in excess of the requirements of the colony and in such narrow ways as to preclude their seeking employment beyond its limits, but this redundancy of professional men, competing with one another, has evidently fostered the litigious disposition of the people. In the legal as in the other professions, if their members were so educated as to be able, in default of honourable and lucrative employment at home, to look for it abroad, the advantage both to themselves and to their neighbours would be considerable. The first step towards such an improvement upon the present state of things would be to secure their education in English, and the strongest inducement thereto, as well as a powerful stimulus to the general enlightenment of the people, would consist in the adoption of English instead of Italian as the language of the Law Courts. As at present, however, very few members of the legal profession, in any of its grades, have an adequate knowledge of English and most of them are entirely ignorant of it, this change can only be gradually brought about. Even if competent lawyers could at present be found among the English-speaking members of the profession, it would be very unjust to their less educated colleagues, many of whom now hold the highest rank in the profession, to debar them from practice on account of their ignorance of a language which in their youth there was no necessity for them to learn. I can only recommend, therefore, though this I do most earnestly, that an early period be fixed by law at which it will be allowable for legal proceedings to be conducted in English instead of in Italian, and that a further period, say of twelve or fifteen years hence, be fixed, after which English shall be the only language allowed to be used in the Law Courts, except of course in taking the evidence of witnesses, and in securing to those Maltese who speak no language but their own a full and satisfactory administration of justice. My object in all the foregoing recommendations is not to interfere with such use as the Maltese people prefer to make of their mother tongue; but as that tongue is not adapted for exclusive adoption or for written communications, to urge that, as far as is consistent with the liberty of the people, English, instead of Italian shall be employed as its auxiliary. in the Law Courts;

317. Great benefit would undoubtedly result from a knowledge of English being possessed by the Catholic clergy in the colony, and from their recognition of the advantages to be brought within reach of their flocks by their being instructed in the language. I do not see my way, however, to do more than recommend that a sufficient acquaintance with English shall be required from all the clergymen presented by the Government to the benefices in its gift, or employed by it as chaplains and in other capacities, as well as from all other professional officials. and among the Clergy.

REFUND OF CUSTOMS DUTIES.

Refund of Customs Duties.

Drawbacks and the Military Contribution.

318. The only remaining question on which I was directed to report—described in Mr. Herbert's letter as "the subject of the drawback allowed to the Imperial Government on account of corn and cattle consumed by the garrison and the fleet"—appears to me so simple that I hope I shall be excused for treating it only very briefly.

319. Upon the average of the past ten years, upwards of £6000 is annually surrendered by the local Government in exempting from duty certain imported articles consumed by Her Majesty's land and sea forces in the island. Of these articles the most important are wheat and bullocks, drawback being allowed only on what is paid for out of the Imperial Exchequer. Everything else liable to duty, though consumed by the forces, is rated on the same conditions as apply to the public. The drawback is thus nothing more nor less than an indirect and variable contribution from local funds towards the maintenance of the Imperial forces.

320. The practice doubtless originated in a desire to avoid the anomaly, as well as the unnecessary expense, of the Exchequer taxing itself for its own support; and, under the former system of colonial government, when deficiencies in local revenue were made good by the parent state, and there was thus, practically, one common purse, it was probably wise and proper. It appears to me, however, to be quite incompatible with the present altered policy of Imperial administration, which not only throws upon colonial governments the entire responsibility of managing their own finances and producing an equilibrium between revenue and expenditure, but also requires from them contributions towards their military defence.

321. The contribution avowedly made by the people of Malta to that object is at present only £5000 a year, a sum which I presume was fixed by Her Majesty's Government rather as an enforcement of a general principle applicable to all Crown Colonies than with the intention of requiring the island to render any substantial assistance towards protecting it from invasion. In the present day of heavy armaments, it would of course be impossible for the Maltese people, by any resources or strength of their own, to defend their island from foreign attacks, and, if they were left to themselves, they would probably incur no expense in making so useless an attempt. It is well understood, moreover, that the English forces, which are stationed in the island in considerable numbers, as well as the fortifications that are maintained at heavy cost, are part of the general policy of the State and not designed at all for the defence or benefit of the Maltese, and this appears to have been practically acknowledged by the Imperial Government in calling for so small a military contribution as £5000 a year. Had there been any intention of exacting a larger sum on that account from the inhabitants, I feel assured that it would have been done openly, and I believe that the present augmentation of it, to the extent of about £6000 a year, is an accident which was not contemplated when the amount of the contribution was fixed.

322. If Her Majesty's Government is now of opinion that the people of Malta should contribute, not £5000, but £11,000 a year, towards its maintenance as a military station, it would certainly be preferable that the increased charge should be made in an open and direct manner. I hope, however, that it is not so. Considering the poverty of the island, and seeing that no sum which the local Government could pay towards its defence would either be at all adequate to the purpose, or a more complete acknowledgment of the principle involved than is made at present, I feel persuaded that it would be no less just than politic on the part of Her Majesty's Government to relinquish all right to drawback, without seeking for any enlargement of the present military contribution.

SUMMARY OF SUGGESTIONS.

Summary of Suggestions.

323. Reverting to the principal object of my visit to Malta, I may now briefly sum up the chief suggestions which I have made as to changes and reductions in its Civil Establishments.

The Governor's Establishment.

324. I am of opinion that, so long as the duties of Commander of the Forces are assigned to the Governor of the Colony, the local contribution towards his official income should be reduced by £2000 a year, that amount being charged to the Imperial Government as an equivalent for his military services. The changes which I have suggested in the management of the gardens adjoining his residences at Sant' Antonio and Verdala ought to lead to a saving of about £330 a year.

325. On the appointment of a successor to the present Chief Secretary, the salary attached to the office may, I consider, be reduced by £300 a year. The modifications of work which I have suggested will enable his Department to dispense with at least one Clerk. SUMMARY OF SUGGESTIONS.
The Chief Secretary's Office.

326. I recommend that the Treasury, as a separate office, be abolished, and its work absorbed in the Receiver-General's Department which I propose to establish. The services of the Cashier, with a salary of £350, and of two Clerks may thus be dispensed with. By investing in Consols the large balance now lying idle in the Treasury chest, the revenue of the island may be augmented by upwards of £1350 a year. The Treasury.

327. I propose that the Land Revenue and Public Works Department be reconstituted as two separate branches of the Public Service;—the Receiver-General's Department, under a Receiver-General who will draw the salary, without allowances, now assigned to the Collector of Land Revenue, and who will also be responsible for the work hitherto done by the Treasury; and the Public Works Department, under a Superintendent, with a salary of £300 a year, whose appointment will render unnecessary the further employment of a Chief Land Surveyor, at £240 a year. The working expenses of the new Departments ought to be less than those of the Departments superseded by them, while I have roughly estimated the increase of land revenue which ought to result from the reforms I have suggested at £6000 a year, and there ought also to be considerable economy in the execution of repairs to public buildings and the construction of new works. The Land Revenue and Public Works Department.

328. The most important suggestion I have had to make with regard to the well-managed Customs Department is that, as a partial set-off to the expense of collecting the revenue, very moderate additions be made to the present charges for store-rent and port dues, the aggregate of which may be estimated at nearly £2000 a year. I consider that one Clerk from this Department may be dispensed with. The Customs Department.

329. At least £1000 a year ought also to be added to the revenue by the fees which I recommend should be charged for bills of health, licences to pontoons and cargo boats, and other documents now issued gratuitously by the Superintendent of Ports. To that officer, in my opinion, should be assigned the control of the Marine Police Force, now under the Superintendent of Police. The Port Department.

330. I also propose that the Superintendent of Police be relieved of the nominal control of the professional staff known as Medical Police. These curtailments of his responsibility will justify a reduction by £100 of the salary attached to his office, and also the removal of two Clerks from the Department. For various licences now granted by, or on the authority of, the Superintendent, small fees should be charged, so as at any rate to defray the cost of issue. The Police Department.

331. I have recommended several modifications in the machinery for the administration of justice. I consider that the functions of the Syndics or Country Magistrates should be to a great extent assimilated to those of the City Magistrates, that the present number of fifteen, in both classes, should be reduced by five, and that those who remain should have the prospect of obtaining higher salaries, with a net gain to the public of about £800 a year. The Magistracies.

332. I also propose to reduce the number of Superior Courts from five to three, without, however, at present reducing the number of Judges. The Superior Courts.

333. By the amalgamation of all the Court Registries and the Public Registry in one General Registry, and a thorough reorganization of the business now done in them, I am of opinion that more than half the number of Clerks now employed therein, as well as many other subordinates, may be dispensed with. The direct economy to be thus secured will be considerable, and the advantage resulting from the improved mode of collecting Court fees and the revision of legal tariffs, which I have suggested, ought to be much greater. The Registries.

334. On the retirement of the present occupants of the offices, I am of opinion that the salary of the Crown Advocate may be reduced by £50; that the separate post of an Advocate for the Poor may be abolished; and that great improvements may be effected in the positions of the Reporters, the Government Notary, and several other legal auxiliaries of the Courts, who are now improperly reckoned as Civil Servants. The Crown Advocate, Advocate for the Poor, Reporters, Government Notary, &c.

335. The same remark applies to the large number of other professional men, physicians, surgeons, land surveyors, &c., who hold the anomalous position of at the same time being on the fixed establishment, with a claim to pension, and having the right to carry on their several callings for their private advantage. By the gradual correction of the abuses which, in this respect, have grown up, great savings, both in salaries and in pensions, may be effected, and the Civil Service may be ultimately rendered far Other Professional Auxiliaries.

SUMMARY OF SUGGESTIONS.	more compact and efficient than it is at present, or can be made to be for some years to come.
The Clerical Establishment.	336. Having recommended several reductions in the clerical strength of different Departments, I have felt it right to suggest that the smaller staff of Clerks who will ultimately be comprised in the Civil Establishment should derive most of the pecuniary benefit that will thus be secured. I propose that their scales of salaries and their prospects of promotion be considerably improved. I anticipate, however, that when the changes are completed, the saving to the Government under this head will be not less than between £800 and £900 per annum.
Minor Reforms.	337. Without recapitulating the numerous minor reforms in the various Departments which I have proposed, I may say that I believe their general effect will conduce greatly to the satisfactory and economical performance of the business of the Government.
The Post Office.	338. If equitable arrangements can be made for the transfer of the Malta Post Office, which is now an Imperial establishment, to the local authorities, I believe that a saving to the Colony of more than £1600 a year ought to result.
Aggregate of Proposed Economies.	339. From the changes and reductions which I have recommended, I anticipate that an annual saving of considerably more than £3000 a year will be effected under the head of salaries, in addition to the £2000 towards the Governor's income which I suggest should be contributed by the Imperial instead of by the local Government. I estimate the addition to the revenue which ought to result from improved management of the Government property in lands and houses, from a revised system of charges for licences, judicial fees, and various services now gratuitously rendered to the public by the Government, and from the local working of the Post Office, at upwards of £11,000 a year. Should Her Majesty's Government consent to abandon the system of drawbacks which is now in force, there will be a further gain of about £6000 a year to the Colony. This latter amount, however, would be subject to reduction in the event of Mr. Rowsell's recommendations for the abolition of the duty on wheat being carried out. If the above figures are correct, they show a total annual saving to the Local Exchequer, including about £8000 contributed or surrendered by the Imperial Government, of at least £22,000, or nearly one-sixth of its entire revenue upon the average of the past few years.
	340. As many of the changes I have recommended will necessitate slight alterations in existing laws, it is desirable that, in the event of their being sanctioned, no time should be lost in taking the requisite legislative action.
Conclusion.	341. In conclusion I may be allowed to acknowledge my indebtedness to the members of the Government and the Civil Service of Malta, as well as to many other gentlemen upon whose courtesy and candour I had no official claim, for the invaluable assistance which they rendered me in the course of my prolonged and, to them, I fear, somewhat irksome inquiries, and to express a hope that the recommendations I have made, if they meet with your approval, may conduce to the prosperity of an Island which holds so important a place among the possessions of the Crown, and the loyalty and industry of whose inhabitants entitle it to such favourable consideration.

I have the honour to be, Sir,
Your most obedient servant,

PENROSE G. JULYAN.

The Right Hon. Sir MICHAEL E. HICKS BEACH, Bart; M.P.
*Her Majesty's Principal Secretary of State
for the Colonies, Downing Street.*

APPENDICES.

APPENDIX A.

Letter of Instructions.

Downing Street, *October 12th*, 1878.

Sir,

With reference to previous correspondence respecting your mission to Malta, I am directed by the Secretary of State for the Colonies to indicate briefly the principal points to which he desires to direct your attention and upon which he wishes to receive your report.

The primary object of your inquiry will, of course, as you are aware, be the organisation and working of the Civil Establishments of the Colony, other than those connected with Education, which will be reported upon by Mr. Keenan, with a view to ascertaining whether it may be practicable, without detriment to the efficient conduct of public business, to effect any reduction in the numbers and cost of the employés in the public service.

But in addition to this principal question, Sir Michael Hicks Beach will be glad to be favoured with your views, after due investigation and consideration, upon the following subjects:—

1. How far it will be desirable to promote the use of English as the official language of the Colony, whether in the Council of Government, in the Courts of Justice, or in other Government proceedings and correspondence. I am to transmit for your information copies of correspondence which had passed on this subject.

2. It has on more than one occasion been proposed in the Council of Government that the salary of the Governor of Malta from local sources should be reduced from £5000 to £3000, the balance, if necessary, being made up from Imperial funds. The ground upon which this proposition has been urged is that the Governor, holding as he now does both the chief military and civil command, can only give a portion of his time to his civil duties, and that the Colony should not therefore be called upon to pay the whole of his salary. This question is one which Sir Michael Hicks Beach wishes you carefully to consider and report upon, and in connection with it he will be glad to know whether, in your opinion, the salary of the Chief Secretary will, on the occurrence of a vacancy in the office, admit of reduction, looking to the importance of the office, and the necessity of its being filled by an officer of experience and ability.

3. Another point to which Sir Michael Hicks Beach desires your attention is one which has been much discussed in the island; viz. the subject of the drawback allowed to the Imperial Government on account of corn and cattle consumed by the Garrison and the Fleet. The question was touched upon by Mr. Rowsell in his report on the Taxation of Malta; but, as it hardly came within the strict limits of his inquiry, he did not consider or discuss it with sufficient care and fulness to enable Her Majesty's Government to come to any decision with respect to it. I am therefore to request that you will examine this question, and lay the case before Her Majesty's Government in such shape as may render it possible to arrive at a settlement.

It will, of course, be satisfactory to the Secretary of State to receive from you any expressions of opinion or suggestions relating to the civil administration of the island generally, which your experience may enable you to offer.

I am, Sir,

Your most obedient servant,

ROBERT G. W. HERBERT.

Sir Penrose Julyan, K.C.M.G.

APPENDIX B.

GOVERNMENT PROPERTY IN LANDS AND HOUSES.

EXCLUSIVE of the property retained by the Imperial authorities, and that let on perpetual lease, the Government owns rural property covering 10,002 acres out of the 59,557 acres comprising the area of the island of Malta, and 1617 acres in Gozo, which has an area of 15,827 acres, besides the whole of the small rocky islands of Comino, Filfla, and Selmone whose respective areas are 688, 48, and 39 acres. This Government property is coloured red in the Plan facing p. 8 of this Report. It is classified in the Government accounts under the headings of "The Crown Property" and "The Property of the Pious Foundations."

I.

THE CROWN PROPERTY—besides several public buildings, as well as others yielding rent, which were lately constructed out of the revenue of the island, and grounds granted on long leases for the construction of dwellings or for agricultural purposes—consists of the property which was held by the Government of the Order of St. John of Jerusalem. The bulk of it appertained to the "Langues" or nationalities to which the Knights of the Order belonged, and its rental was to be appropriated to the maintenance of the Knights and of the auberges and churches owned by them. It was accordingly divided, according to the claims of the several Langues, as follows:—(1) Provence; (2) Auvergne; (3) France; (4) Italy; (5) Aragon; (6) Germany; (7) Castile; (8) England. Beside these, there were several separate endowments or foundations, intended for special purposes, concerning which the following details have been furnished to me by the Land Revenue Department.

1. The Property of the "Fondazione Lascaris" was granted to the Government of the Order, between 1647 and 1655, by the Grand Master Lascaris; the object of the grant was to appropriate the rent of that property for the purchase of 3000 muskets; for the keeping of two galleys; for the construction and repair of fortifications; for the purchase of 5000 cantars of saltpetre, to be converted into gunpowder in case of a siege; and for the yearly purchase of "miglio," up to 8000 salms, to be kept in store, for use in the event of a siege.

2. The property of the "Fondazione Caraffa" was left to the Government by the Grand Master Caraffa, with the burden of a legacy of 50 sc. (£4 3s. 4d.) payable yearly to the Convent of the Minori Conventuali.

3. The property of the "Fondazione Carnero," was left by the Vice-Chancellor Gaspare Carnero, with a burden of 90 sc. (£7.10s.) per annum for a benefice for three priests who were to perform service in the Church della Vittoria.

4. The property of the "Fondazione Perellos" was left by the Grand Master Perellos, with the burden of a mass to be said on all feasts of obligation in the Chapel of San Salvator at the Marina; with another burden of keeping a lamp constantly lighted in the choir of St. John's Church; and another burden of defraying the necessary expenses for solemnising the Feast of San Vincenzo Ferreri in St. John's Church.

5. The property of the "Fondazione Paola" was left in 1635 by the Grand Master Paola, in order that its rent might be appropriated for the construction of a galley every five years.

6. The property of the "Fondazione Manoel" was granted in 1724 by the Grand Master Manoel, in order that its rent might be appropriated for the perpetual maintenance of Fort Manoel (built by himself) and of its church and garrison; also for the celebration of masses in St. John's Church.

7. The property of the "Fondazione Cotoner" was granted in 1676 by the Grand Master Cotoner, in order that its rent might be appropriated for the maintenance of the garrison of Fort Ricasoli, for the maintenance of the chapel existing in that fort, and for the subsidy of a Chair of Surgery and Anatomy in the hospital.

8. The property of the "Fondazione Scappi" was left to the Government in 1626 by Caterina Scappi, for the maintenance of an Asylum for poor women suffering from incurable complaints. That Fondazione was subsequently endowed by other persons.

9. The property of the "Fondazione Passalacqua" was left by Cesare Passalacqua in 1683 for providing, from its rents, candles and incense for the use of St. John's Church, and for the celebration of masses in that church.

10. The property of the "Fondazione Lomellina" was left in 1681 by the Bali Fra Stefano Maria Lomellina towards meeting, with the rents thereof, the expenses for the performance of religious ceremonies in the Oratory of St. John's Church.

11. The property of the "Fondazione Marradas" was left in 1637 by the Bali Fra Baldassare Marradas, for providing, with its rent, candles for use in St. John's Church.

12. The property of the "Fondazione Assemblea" was left by the Grand Master Lacassiere and others, for the daily performance of Divine Service in St. John's Church, for the celebration of masses in that church, for providing it with wax and candles, and for alms to be distributed amongst the poor; also for the yearly marriage legacies of two poor girls.

13. The property of the "Fondazione Capella della Beata Vergine di Filermo" was left in 1588, by the Knight Scaglia and others, for the celebration of masses in the Chapel of Beata Vergine di Filermo of St. John's Church.

14. The property of the "Fondazione Grotta di San Paolo" was left in 1617 by the Grand Master Alofio di Wignacourt for the formation of a College of Chaplains to perform daily Divine Service in the Church of St. Paul's Grotto at Notabile.

15. The property of the "Fondazione Nibbia" (including the church) was left in 1619 by the Knight Commander Giorgio Nibbia, for providing sacred utensils, and for the maintenance of the Church Nibbia, which was annexed to the cemetery of the Hospital of the Order of St. John of Jerusalem.

16. The property of the "Fondazione Tabone" was left in 1609 by the Reverend Agostino Tabone for the maintenance of the Chaplain of the Church of San Giacomo.

17. The property of the "Fondazione Marulla" was acquired in 1644 by the money left by the Knight Commander Marulla. The rent of that property was to be enjoyed by the Admiral pro temp. of the Order.

18. The property of the "Congregazione di Guerra," consisted of the ground-rents on sites at Floriana and Cottonera, granted by the Government to private individuals for building purposes, rents of redoubts and other parts of the fortifications. Those rents were appropriated by the War Branch of the Government towards the expenses for the defence of the island.

19. The property of the "Congregazione di Gesù" (including the Church del Gesù, and the building at present used as University and Lyceum, also the church and building of San Calcedonio at Floriana) belonged to the Order of St. Ignatius (Jesuits). On their expulsion, in 1768, from Malta, at the instance of the King of Naples, the Church authorities granted the administration of that property to the Grand Master of the Order, with the obligation of forming and subsidising a College and University, and of continuing the performance of Divine Service in the Church of the Gesù, and in that of San Calcedonio at Floriana.

II.

The Pious Foundations (the total revenue from which, according to the Land Revenue Returns for 1877, was £3532 9s. 1¼d.) are divided under the following heads: (1) Monte di Pietà, £89 15s. 4½d.; (2) Redenzione, £1847 4s. 0¼d.; (3) Santo Spirito, £460 11s. 9¾d.; (4) Maddalena, £595 19s. 9¼d.; (5) Cumulo Ordinario; (6) Cumulo Xerri; (7) Cumulo Gatt; (8) Cumulo Barone Inguanez; (9) Cumulo Baronessa Inguanez, (for the last five, £538 18s. 1d.). I have collected the following details as to these foundations:—

1. The "Monte di Pietà" was founded on the 15th of January, 1598, in virtue of a Decree of the General Chapter of the Order held in that year, pursuant to an application made by the Commendatore Fra Emmanuele de Couros, of the Priory of Portugal, and submitted by him to the Grand Master, Fra Martino Garzes, the then reigning Prince of the island, stating the nature of the Institution it was desirable to establish, which was that of "advancing money on pawns at a very low "interest, with the object of putting down the usurious transactions which were at that time practised, "particularly with the poor, by the Jews, and by the slaves." Commendatore De Couros having contributed a small capital, and Commendatore Fra Francesco Moleti a still smaller one, out of their private means, the business of the Charity was commenced. Large grants and subsidies in money were subsequently made to this institution by the Grand Masters Perellos, Zondadari, Manoel, and Pinto, and landed property bequeathed to it by private individuals. Its income was considerably increased by an act of the Grand Master, De Rohan, dated the 18th of September, 1789, which united to it the revenues of the "Monte di Redenzione." In September 1799 this great and wealthy charity was plundered of all its capitals and pawns by the French; but the British Government re-established it in October 1801.

2. The "Monte di Redenzione" was another institution of very great importance. It was founded at the suggestion of a Capuchin Friar, Father Raffaele, who in a sermon preached in the Church of the Grand Masters, during the Lent of 1607, so moved his hearers by his pathetic description of the sufferings of Christian slaves, that the Grand Master, Alofio de Wignacourt, and the knights who were present, at once commenced a collection for the purpose of establishing, without loss of time, the institution delineated by the eloquent preacher, the object of which was that of "providing the "requisite means by which Christians, falling into slavery under the Turks, might be redeemed, "especially if they be poor, and either brothers, knights, or natives of this island." Its funds were soon raised considerably by the large contributions of the knights, and of the inhabitants, many of whom had near relations or dear friends pining in slave-dungeons in Barbary and Constantinople. A commission composed of four Knights (Grand Crosses), two secular inhabitants, and a Capuchin Father, to honour the originators of the Institution, was at once formed, with the Grand Master at its head, for the purpose of encouraging the collections, and managing their application. Subsequent legacies of private individuals, especially that of Catarina Vitali, in 1619, considerably enriched this Institution, the funds of which greatly increased by accumulation as slavery diminished, whilst those of the "Monte di Pietà" had become inadequate to meet the wants of the poor. Amalgamation of the two Institutions was therefore thought expedient, which measure was effected by the Grand Master, De Rohan, on the 18th of September, 1789, and since that date, to the present time, the united

Institutions have assumed the designation of "*Monte di Pietà e Redenzione.*" A marble tablet on the façade of the present building commemorates the event.

3. "Santo Spirito" is the oldest hospital in the island, and its existence dates prior to 1370. It was originally attached to the adjacent Convent of San Francisco; but, at a date unknown, it was separated from it and placed under the "Guirati" of Notabile. On the suppression of that body by Sir Thomas Maitland (see Proclamation No. XI. of the 30th of December, 1818) the whole of the property and other revenues under their control were transferred to the Collector of Land Revenue. This hospital was generously endowed by private individuals. Dr. Philippo Giacomo Gauci, and his wife Vivia, bequeathed considerable property in 1717, and Dr. Saverio Agius made a donation of 12,000 scudi, in 1736.

4. The "Maddalena" was a monastery for the reception of penitent Prostitutes, or Magdalens. It was originally founded by the Grand Master Verdala in 1583, but not endowed by him. It was maintained by grants of money and allowances of wheat and oil by the Common Treasury, and was, in course of time, admitted to a share of all the prizes made by the Navy of the Order. It also received the fifth part of the estate of every prostitute, whose will was not legal and valid unless it contained such a legacy. These precarious revenues, however, were considerably benefited by the permanent addition made to them on the incorporation of the property of Gerolama Ciantar, in November 1646. On the arrival of the French, in 1798, this monastery was suppressed, and converted into a hospital for the male patients of the civil population, that "the Sacred Infirmary of the Order" might be appropriated for the sick of the invading army.

5, 6, 7, 8, and 9. These foundations constitute "the Monte or Cumulo de Carità," which was formed soon after the raising of the great siege of 1565, by the voluntary contributions of the wealthier inhabitants of the island, to relieve the widows and orphans left behind by the brave who fell in that memorable conflict. The sums collected were by the "Giurati" of Notabile invested, and the interest was, for the greater part, distributed annually in marriage portions to a number of native-born-orphan young women (daughters of native parents) to be given in marriage on the festival day of St. Paul. Considerable legacies were, from time to time, bequeathed by private individuals to this "monte" or fund, to be applied for the purpose above stated. But, subsequent to 1618, other legacies were received prescribing different kinds of relief. The fund had consequently to be divided into two branches; one called "Cumulo ordinario," and the other, "Cumulo straordinario." The object of the first continued to be that of granting marriage portions, and that of the second, of providing any other kind of relief. Soon after this date, Baron Gregorio Xerri bequeathed the handsome sum of 30,000 scudi, the interest of which was to be applied partly as marriage portions, and partly in the purchase of wheat to be distributed to the poor on Saint Barnabas' Day. In 1739 the notary, Guiseppe Gatt, left property, the rental of which was also to be devoted to the encouragement of marriages among the poor; and in 1758, the Baroness Diana Testaferrata Inguanez, and in 1761, her husband, the Baron Marcantonio Inguanez, bequeathed large legacies, by which alms, to the amount of 5 scudi per head, could be distributed among the poor of Notabile, and of the villages, Dingli and Tarturni.

III.

The Churches and Chapels at present belonging to the Government are those which were built at the expense either of a League, or of one of the Grand Masters or Knights, and afterwards presented or bequeathed by them to the Order of St. John. Buildings thus left were incorporated with the public property, and, according to the statutes of the Order, placed under the jurisdiction of the Grand Prior, by being affiliated to the Conventual Church. The Grand Prior entrusted these churches or chapels to the Brothers Chaplains of the Order, who acted as their Rectors, and lived in the residences attached to them, where such accommodation was provided by the Founders. The Government took possession of the whole of this property, by right of succession, on the surrender of the island, and with the property the burden was assumed of effecting the necessary repairs, and providing sacred vestments, utensils, and furniture, besides the responsibility and trouble of appointing clergymen to take charge of the same.

I have collected the following information concerning these churches and chapels:

1. The Church of San Giovanni (the conventual church of the Order) in Valletta, is at present used as joint cathedral by the Bishop and Chapters of the Cathedral. The building, fixtures, and furniture only are supplied and kept in repair by the Government, the sacred vestments, vases, and utensils being provided by the officiating Chapters. The Grand Priory and Vice-Priory, residences attached to the church, were given by Government on long leases to private individuals.

2. The Church of Sant' Antonio Abate, commonly called Della Vittoria, in Valletta, near the Auberge de Castille, is the church built by La Vallette to cover the foundation stone of Valletta, and was for some time the parochial church of the Order, before the building of the Church of San Giovanni. It has two residences attached to it. One is occupied by the Rector (formerly the parish priest), and the other by the Sacristan. The Rector receives £30 per annum, but is bound to supply altar-bread and candles for all the masses, and the Sacristan £10, without any obligation except that of keeping the church clean.

3. The Church of the Gesù, formerly belonging to the Fathers of the Society of Jesus, in Strada Mercanti, close to the Palace, is the finest church in Valletta as to architecture. It is used on Sundays by the Catholic soldiers of the garrison. The buildings attached to this church, the former residence of the Fathers, are now occupied by the University and Lyceum of the island. The Rector has an adequate allowance for the wants of this church, but all repairs of building and furniture are attended to by the Government.

4. The Church of Santa Barbara, attached to the Langue de Provence, is in Strada Reale. No residence was originally provided for the rector of this church. It is at present in charge of a congregation, who provide what may be necessary.

5. The Church of Notre Dame de Liesse, attached to the Langue de France, built to commemorate the miracle of Ismeria, the most interesting episode of the battle of Ascalon, is in Strada Marina, near Lascaris Gate. It has a residence for the rector, and all wants are provided for by the Government.

6. The Church of Santa Catarina, attached to the Langue d'Italie, is situated in Strada Mezzodi, near the Auberge de Castille. It has a residence for the rector in Strada Zaccaria, No. 13, in lieu of the original one, transferred to the Military Department.

7. The Church of San Giacomo, attached to the Langue de Castille, is in Strada Mercanti, near the Auberge d' Italie. The residence of this church is occupied by the priests who assist the dying in Valletta. It has lately been rebuilt at the expense of the Government.

8. The Church of San Rocco is in the Strada Santa Ursola. It was built at the expense of the Università in 1592, to commemorate the liberation of the island from the plague of that year. There are rooms connected with the church for the use of the sexton. Being attached to the Church of San Paolo, there may be some doubt whether it is Government property. Public money is occasionally, however, voted for its maintenance, and I find that the Estimates for 1880 contain a vote for repairs to be effected in it.

9. The Church of the Pilar, attached to the Langue d' Aragon, is in the Strada Ponente, near the Auberge d' Aragon. It has a residence for the rector, and another for the sacristan.

10. The Church of Nostra Signora di Pietà, or of Nibbia, attached to the cemetery of the Sacred Infirmary, is near the Hospital for Incurables. The residence is let, as one of the chaplains of the Hospital of Incurables has charge of the church.

11. The Church of the Blessed Saviour, or Del Salvatore, at the Marina, near Pinto's Bonded Warehouses, has a residence which is occupied by the rector.

12. The Church of the Immaculate Conception, commonly called Saura, is near the Public Gardens in Floriana. It has a residence, which is occupied by the rector.

13. The Chapel of San Rocco, for the service of persons in quarantine, is within the Floriana Lines, on St. Michael's Bastion, overlooking the Quarantine Harbour. It has no residence, and is connected with the quarantine establishment.

14. The Church of San Nicola di Bari is in Fort Ricasoli. There are quarters attached to this church, but they are not occupied by the rector.

15. The Church of San Giovanni Elemosinario is in Cospicua, near Sant' Elena Gate. A fine villa and garden are attached to this church, but let to private individuals by the rectors. This property is an ecclesiastical benefice in the gift of the Government.

16. The Church of San Francisco di Paola, at Senglea, on the French Creek, is now naval property. This church is affiliated to the parish church of Senglea, but the Government has some claim upon it.

17. The Church of the Grotto of St. Paul and its adjacent college, in Città Vecchia, is served by a number of clergymen called Chaplains of the Grotto of St. Paul. They form a chapter, and have rooms in the college and a salary from the Government.

18. The Church of San Paolo a Mare, at St. Paul's Bay, has a residence for the rector; but this church, being affiliated to the Church of St. Paul's Grotto at Città Vecchia, is included in the expenditure of the latter.

19. The Chapel of Nostra Signora della Mercede is in the Tower or Palace of Selmone, near St. Paul's Bay. There are rooms for the accommodation of the officiating clergyman, but he does not reside permanently in them.

20. The Church of the Assunta is at the Marsa, near Casal Curmi. It is a small rural chapel, with no residence attached.

21. The Church of San Giovanni Battista, near the village of Siggeui, has a residence for the rector.

22. The Church of Santa Ubaldesca, in Casal Paola, near Corradino Prison, has no residence attached. It is in fact only part of a church, having been left incomplete by the founder, the Grand Master de Paul.

23. The Church of San Silvestro, near the village of Musta, is a rural chapel belonging to the Commenda Fiteni.

24. The Chapel of Sant' Agata, in the Coast Tower of Migiarro. 25. The Chapel of Saint Thomas the Apostle, in the Coast Tower of St. Thomas in Marsa Scala. 26. The Chapel of the Madonna delle Grazie, in the Coast Tower of the Madonna delle Grazie. 27. The Chapel of San Luciano, in the fort of San Luciano at Marsa Scirocco. These chapels are all abandoned, except the last named. There are no quarters for the chaplains or rectors in any of them.

28. Another Chapel of the Madonna delle Grazie is in Fort Chambray, Gozo. No quarters are attached to it. The rector resides at Rabato.

29. The Chapel of San Giovanni Battista, in the Marsa il Forno, Gozo, is very much frequented in summer, when the inhabitants of Rabato repair to this bay for bathing.

30. A Church of Santa Maria is in the small creek of Santa Maria, Comino. There is no residence attached to this church. The rector does not live at Comino, but crosses the water from Gozo.

APPENDIX C.

OBSERVATIONS ON THE JUDICIAL AND MAGISTERIAL ESTABLISHMENTS OF MALTA, BY SIR ANTONIO MICALLEF, K.C.M.G., LL.D., PRESIDENT OF HER MAJESTY'S COURT OF APPEAL.

I.

Sindaci e Magistrati della Polizia Giudiziaria di Malta.

1. Il numero dei Sindaci, come è stabilito coll' Ordinanza N° XI del 1839, mi sembra eccessivo.
2. Il numero dei Sindaci può essere limitato a cinque, nel caso di vacanza per promozione od altrimenti, e fatta una equa distribuzione dei distretti della campagna.
3. L' ufficio dei detti cinque Sindaci, in quanto che questi sono capi dei distretti, ed incaricati dei doveri della polizia da essere anche da loro sorvegliati, come ufficiali superiori, e degli atti dello stato civile, ai termini delle sezioni 6 e 7 della Ordinanza N° XI del 1839, ed in conformità alle disposizioni del Proclama N° III del 31 Gennaio 1816, dell' Ordinanza N° I del 1873 (articoli 157 e 273 e seguenti), come pure di altre leggi criminali e di polizia e dei regolamenti in vigore specialmente per oggetti sanitari, per lo stato delle strade e pel sollievo dei poveri, ecc., dovrà a mio credere essere mantenuto e conservato—specialmente perchè per l' adempimento dei detti doveri sarà necessario incaricare altre persone, e le quali non potranno essere di soddisfazione al pubblico come al presente sono i Sindaci— di professione avvocati—oltre che la sostituzione di altre persone sarà a recare una eguale spesa, per non dire maggiore, a danno del pubblico in generale.
4. L' ufficio dei detti sindaci, come ufficiali giudiziari, dev' essere anche conservato (vedansi gli articoli 72 e 136 delle Leggi di Org. e Proc. Civile, gli articoli 317, 332 e 382 delle Leggi Criminali, e gli articoli 361, 362, 363, 364, 365 e 371 della Ordinanza N° VII del 1868). Se l' ufficio dei detti sindaci, come autorità giudiziaria, sarà abolito, sarà necessario incaricare degli attuali loro doveri giudiziari almeno due Magistrati della Polizia Giudiziaria—il che necessariamente dovrà avere l' effetto della necessità di non potersi diminuire l' attuale numero dei detti Magistrati, senza alcun vantaggio della cassa pubblica, ma anche con danno della stessa, e del pubblico in generale—per la ragione—che sarà necessario costringere le parti, per un tenue oggetto in lite, allontanarsi dai luoghi del loro distretto e fare trasportare in un luogo diverso i loro testimoni, con perdita di tempo e di lavoro, ed anche con aggravio di spese.
5. Si deve notare che Sir Thomas Maitland riconoscendo il danno che veniva a soffrire la popolazione col costringerla a litigare per tenui oggetti in luoghi distanti dalla propria residenza, aveva saviamente organizzato dei tribunali locali, con una limitata giurisdizione per affari civili, col suo Proclama del 31 Gennaio 1816—e che i detti tribunali locali, con varie modificazioni fatte posteriormente, furono conservati in vigore, e pel lungo corso di più di anni 60, con vantaggio del pubblico in generale—ed in quanto è in mia cognizione, senza che sul proposito vi sia stata alcuna lagnanza.
6. Anzi io direi che per poter essere diminuito il numero attuale dei Magistrati della Polizia Giudiziaria si dovrebbe estendere la giurisdizione dei detti cinque Sindaci, come ufficiali giudiziari, collo autorizzarli.

1° A poter prendere cognizione di tutte le contravvenzioni commesse nei loro rispettivi distretti, e non già alle sole contravvenzioni contemplate nell' Ordinanza N° XV del 1859. La detta estensione di giurisdizione sarà ad arrecare un notabile vantaggio alla cassa pubblica, perchè avrà per effetto una diminuzione notabile della somma che al presente si spende per citazioni e spese di testimoni e di trasporto degli stessi nelle Corti dei Magistrati della Valletta—come pure per spese di trasporto dei connestabili e per vettura all' ufficiale di Polizia che dovesse presentare le cause innanzi la Corte.

2° Coll' autorizzare i detti Sindaci a tenere gli accessi contemplati negli articoli 460, 461 e 465 delle Leggi Criminali, colla assistenza del proprio Registratore e ciò nel caso in cui non vi fosse ancora alcun rapporto, denunzia o querela contro alcun individuo, come autore o complice nel reato. La detta estensione sarà a diminuire le spese che si fanno dai detti Magistrati per gli accessi ed esenterà il Registratore di detti Magistrati od il suo assistente o scrivano dai doveri impostigli col detto articolo e dall' allontanarsi dall' ufficio senza attendere al altri doveri.

3° Coll' incaricarli della visita degli Atti Notariali (Ord. V. del 1855), dei Notari residenti nei loro distretti.

7. Se saranno adottati i detti provvedimenti si potrà facilmente sopprimere l' ufficio di uno e forse due dei Magistrati della Polizia Giudiziaria, e così si avrà il risparmio almeno del salario di due Sindaci, colla proporzionata rata delle *allowances* e *contingencies*, del salario di uno o due Magistrati della Polizia, di due Registratori e di una buona porzione della somma che si suole annualmente votare per citazioni e spese di testimoni e per spese di accessi nelle Corti della Polizia Giudiziaria di Malta per la Valletta.

8. L' attuale giurisdizione civile, si dei Magistrati che dei Sindaci non dovrebbe essere estesa—per la ragione che se avrà luogo la detta estensione le parti con difficoltà potrebbero prevalersi dell' assistenza di buoni avvocati, i quali senza alcun dubbio saranno a ricusare di lasciare le loro occupazioni nelle Corti Superiori per comparire innanzi ai detti ufficiali—e per la ragione che è assai questionabile se in pratica la detta estensione sarà a recare un reale vantaggio al pubblico, il quale forse non è disposto ad avere quella fiducia nei Magistrati e nei Sindaci per cause eccedenti il valore di £5 che al presente ha verso i Giudici di S. M., assistiti da avvocati.

9. Solamente suggerirei che le cause decise dai Magistrati e dai Sindaci fino ad una data somma— p. e. di una o due lire sterline—fossero dichiarate inappellabili, come Sir Thomas Maitland aveva col Proclama del 15 Ottobre 1817 dichiarato senza appello le sentenze dei Magistrati del Gozo fino a scudi venti.

10. Pel caso in cui gli affari nelle Corti Inferiori per la moltiplicità o per legittimi impedimenti de' Magistrati, specialmente contemporanei, non potranno essere definiti convenientemente e senza ritardi indebiti nella amministrazione della giustizia, io suggerirei che il Capo del Governo Civile dovesse avere l'autorità di ordinare, per via di Notificazione del Governo, ad uno o più Sindaci per turno, di agire da Magistrati della Polizia Giudiziaria, per tutti gli affari di attribuzione delle loro Corti, si civili che criminali, a ciò per un periodo di tempo limitato o determinato, e durante il bisogno e fino la cessazione dell' impedimento dei Magistrati. Se si addotterà il detto provvedimento non vi potrà essere mai alcun inconveniente per la diminuzione dal numero dei Magistrati.

(Valletta, 16 Decembre 1878.)

II.

Corte dei Magistrati della Polizia Giudiziaria in Seconda Istanza.

1. I doveri attribuiti coll'articolo 65 delle Leggi di Organizzazione e Procedura Civile alla Corte dei Magistrati per l'isola di Malta, costituita in seconda istanza con tre Magistrati, possono essere adempiti dalla Corte di Appello di S. M. come si eseguivano prima della promulgazione delle dette leggi, secondo il Proclama del 27 Febbrajo 1839, ed altre leggi al presente abrogate.
2. Per la decisione delle dette cause nella Corte di Appello non è necessario l'intervento dei tre Giudici di questa Corte—e niente osta perchè possa prenderne cognizione uno dei membri della detta Corte, compreso il Presidente, e per turno—ad eccezione del caso in cui il Giudice sedente per turno opini, che avuto riguardo all'importanza della questione gli sia necessaria la assistenza degli altri suoi colleghi.
3. Forse sarà anche spediente esaminare, se sia necessaria la Corte de' Magistrati della Polizia Giudiziaria per le isole Gozo e Comino, costituita in seconda istanza, giusta l'articolo 66 delle dette leggi.
4. E nel caso di unione della detta Corte in Seconda Istanza per le isole del Gozo e Comino alla Corte di Appello in Malta, io prenderei la libertà di suggerire, che per risparmio di spese e di protilazione nei Giudizi l'esame dei testimoni residenti nel Gozo si potesse fare anche nel Gozo, per mezzo di un supplente residente nel Gozo e da nominarsi, secondo le occorrenze, dalla Corte di Appello—quante volte i litiganti o qualcuno dei litiganti non stimeranno o non stimerà proprio di fare esaminare *viva voce* i detti testimoni in Malta, a proprie spese—o la Corte di Malta non riputerà di ufficio necessario l'esame a *viva voce*.

(Valletta, 16 Decembre 1878.)

III.

Dei Giudici di Sua Maestà.

1. Secondo la Costituzione delle Corti pubblicata nel 1814 il numero dei Giudici di S. M. era di sei, oltre il Presidente dell' Alta Corte di Appello. Il detto numero di sette Giudici col Proclama del 27 Febbraio 1839 con cui fu promulgata l'Ordinanza N° III del 1839, sulle raccomandazioni dei Regi Commissionari d'inchiesta, fu limitato a sei, compreso il detto Presidente. E sebbene la detta Ordinanza del 1839 fu abrogata in toto coll' articolo 1023 delle Leggi di Organizzazione e Procedura Civile, e sebbene coll'articolo 5 delle dette Leggi non fu determinato il numero dei Giudici di S. M., è certo però, che, secondo la consuetudine il numero di sei Giudici, compreso il Presidente, non fu mai alterato.
2. Secondo la mia opinione l'attuale numero dei Giudici, compreso il Presidente, non è eccessivo, e la limitazione di quel numero, se avrà luogo, dovrà necessariamente dopo alcuni mesi cagionare dei ritardi assai dannosi nella amministrazione della giustizia, specialmente nel caso di infermità od altro legittimo impedimento di due o più Giudici destinati a sedere in una Corte.
3. A mio credere sarebbe un errore il conchiudere quanto dovrebbe essere il numero dei Giudici da un argomento desunto del numero delle cause che si introducono annualmente nelle Corti di Giustizia Superiori, perchè è certissimo che la importanza delle cause non dipende dal numero dei processi e delle domande, ma dalla gravità delle questioni che si sottomettono al decidente.
4. Sarebbe anche erroneo, come penso, argomentare per la diminuzione del numero dei Giudici dalla durata del tempo che i Giudici occupano nelle sedute pubbliche, perchè le questioni difficili, e le quali non sono rare, necessariamente si devono studiare e risolvere nella quiete e nella solitudine, e sarebbe assai difficile, in una buona porzione dei casi, motivare in iscritto e convenientemente le sentenze, nel fatto e nel dritto, come prescrivono gli articoli 244, 245, 246 e 247 delle dette Leggi, e senza un serio e maturo esame in privato e senza una occupazione ben lunga, in certi casi, per ore ed ore. Aggiungasi a questo, che l'ommissione di una buona motivazione, come di legge, oltre che può influire seriamente sull' amministrazione della giustizia, espone il decidente al rischio di vedere rovesciata la sentenza col rimedio dell' appello, od anche con quello della ritrattasione nei casi preveduti nell'articolo 828 delle dette Leggi, quando anche si tratti di sentenza di seconda istanza. (Inciso 3 del detto Articolo).
5. Nè per l'oggetto di limitare il numero dei Giudici si potrebbe, come opino, estendere i poteri del Capo del Governo Civile datigli coll' articolo 12 delle dette Leggi di poter nominare uno o più Giudici supplenti, anche pel caso di moltiplicità di affari e di infermità contemporanea di più Giudici di S. M. perchè il rimedio non sarebbe adottabile, per ovvie ragioni, specialmente perchè il pubblico ed il foro non sarebbe ad avere alcuna fiducia in Giudici temporanei per due o tre mesi, senza alcuna garanzia per la loro indipendenza, e con certezza che da tutti sarebbero ad essere considerati come aspiranti ad una giudicatura a vita.
6. Nè anche sono di opinione che per l'oggetto di limitare il numero dei Giudici di S. M. si potrebbe restringere l'attuale loro giurisdizione, perchè prima di adottare un provvedimento di

questa specie si dovrebbe seriamente pensare a chi si dovrebbe attribuire la giurisdizione che si toglierebbe ai Giudici, perchè sarebbe difficile di persuadere i litiganti a riporre in altra persona la fiducia che di ordinario hanno nei Giudici, scelti da tra i migliori avvocati ed ufficiali indipendenti e durante la loro vita—e perchè i litiganti innanzi alle Corti Inferiori non potranno mai avere quella assistenza che hanno, mediante l'opera di buoni avvocati, nelle Corti Superiori.

Io, per altro, per una più equa distribuzione degli affari nelle Corti Superiori e per evitare non necessari ritardi nell'amministrazione della giustizia per parte dei sei Giudici di S. M. suggerirei:

1° Che tre dei Giudici di Sua Maestà dovessero sedere per turno in prima istanza, sia che l'attuale Corte di Commercio sarà unita alla Corte Civile, sia che sarà conservata l'attuale organizzazione della detta Corte di Commercio.

2° Che gli altri tre Giudici di S. M., compreso il Presidente della Corte di Appello, dovessero sedere non solo nella Corte di Appello e nella Corte Criminale composta di tre Giudici, ma anche, e per turno, negli affari di volontaria giurisdizione, sia che l'attuale Seconda Aula Civile sarà unita alla Corte di Appello, sia che la detta Second'Aula sarà conservata come al presente, come pure dovessero sedere, anche per turno, nella Corte Criminale, quando è composta di un solo Giudice, secondo il regolamento interno che in quanto al turno saranno a fare si i Giudici di prima che di seconda istanza, e salvo il disposto nella seconda parte dell'articolo 10 e dello articolo 11 delle dette Leggi.

3° Che le cause di ritrattazione contemplate nel detto articolo 828 e seguenti dovessero essere proposte dinanzi alla Corte di Appello solamente, anche quando si trattasse di sentenze di prima istanza, ed innanzi ai Giudici ordinari di seconda istanza, compreso il Presidente, anche nei casi nei quali questi tre Giudici avessero deciso le cause di cui si domandasse la ritrattazione, e ciò, in conformità all'opinione prevalente prima della promulgazione delle dette Leggi nei casi di restituzione in intero e nei quali, come insegnavano molti dottori, la causa si dovea proporre in appello e d anche innanzi gli stessi Giudici che la avessero decisa; opinione, la quale fu spesso adottata in pratica dal mio dotto e compianto predecessore Sir Paolo Dingli.

7. Io ancora, per l'oggetto di fare diminuire i casi ai quali si suole ricorrere all'esame testimoniale, con ritardi nell'amministrazione della giustizia e con una conseguente non necessaria occupazione dei Giudici, suggerirei che nelle cause relative a promesse di matrimonii, la promessa potesse essere solamente provata per atto pubblico o scrittura privata, e non già per mezzo di testimonii.

(Valletta, 16 Decembre 1878.)

IV.

Corte di Commercio di Sua Maestà.

1. Mi pare che sarà utile la soppressione della Corte di Commercio di S. M. come è al presente organizzata cogli articoli 45 e seguenti delle Leggi di Organizzazione e Procedura Civile e cogli articoli 317 e seguenti dell'Ordinanza Num. XIII. del 1857—e la giurisdizione della attuale Corte di Commercio può essere attribuita, senza alcun inconveniente e danno del pubblico, alla Corte Civile di Sua Maestà, come è in genere contemplata nell'inciso primo dello articolo primo delle dette Leggi di Org. e Proc. Civile.

2. È in sin da tempo cessata la ragione per cui fu introdotto presso di noi il tribunale eccezionale di commercio—e quindi la distinzione tra la giurisdizione civile e la commerciale. La Corte di Commercio, come distinta dalla Civile, fu conservata anche da Sir Thomas Maitland colla costituzione delle Corti di Giustizia, pubblicata nel 1814, sul fondamento—che i giudici della Corte di Commercio erano commercianti di professione—sebbene assistiti in prima istanza da un Giudice di S. M. ed in seconda istanza da due Giudici di S. M.

3. Al presente le cause commerciali si decidono, si in prima che in seconda istanza, dai soli Giudici di S. M., come siedono nelle Corti Civili e nelle cause civili. E sebbene è vero, che anche secondo la legge in vigore può essere chiesto dalle parti, in certi casi, l'intervento dei Consoli nelle Corti di Giurisdizione Commerciale, non però meno certo che in pratica la detta legge—in sin da anni—non è in osservanza e non si domanda mai l'intervento dei Consoli, di modo che, in tutti i casi, le cause commerciali, al presente, si decidono dai Giudici di S. M. solamente—come si giudicano nelle Corti di Giurisdizione Civile.

4. Come è organizzata attualmente la Corte di Commercio spesso insorgono questioni sulla competenza della Corte, a domanda delle parti ed anche *ex officio*, resolubili secondo le regole stabilite negli articoli 260, 748, 782, 783, 784, 785 e 786 delle dette leggi, questioni inutili e le quali saranno senza dubbio evitate se cesserà la distinzione tra la giurisdizione civile e la commerciale.

5. Egli è vero che secondo la legge in vigore i termini legali, anche nel caso di appello, nei casi commerciali sono minori di quei che sono stabiliti per gli affari civili (vedansi gli articoli 151, 163, 252, 266 e 273 delle dette leggi); ma la detta differenza tra i termini è al certo inutile; e nei casi di urgenza la Corte può abbreviare i termini ed applicare indistintamente le disposizioni degli articoli 122, 178, 193, e 271 delle dette Leggi.

6. Nel caso di unione della Corte di Commercio alla Corte Civile tutti gli impiegati nel Registro della detta Corte Commerciale potranno essere trasferiti al Registro della Corte Civile. E nel caso di vacanza, per promozione, od altrimenti, dell'attuale Registratore della detta Corte di Commercio, del suo assistente, del Maresciallo e dello Scrivano No. 3 in quel Registro, non sarà necessaria la nomina di altre persone in loro vece; perchè a mio credere gl'impiegati attualmente nel Registro civile, uniti a quei che vi saranno trasferiti dal Registro Commerciale, sono bastanti per adempiere i doveri dei due Registri uniti, anche senza le persone che come ho detto non sarà necessario di sostituire, nel caso di vacanza per promozione od altrimenti.

7. Nel caso della detta unione sarà anche necessario verificare se sia eccessiva la somma in tutto di lire sterline cento e sedici per anno che attualmente si suole pagare per legatura di libri piccole

spese, e *stationery* nei due Registri, e se sia sufficiente pel solo Registro Civile, quantunque unito al Commerciale, una somma minore.

8. Pel caso di servizi urgenti e straordinarj, e per l'adempimento dei quali il Registratore della Corte Civile riputasse non essere sufficiente, senza loro aggravio, la opera degli impiegati nel suo Registro, io suggerirei :

1° Che il detto Registratore dovesse essere autorizzato a prevalersi della opera degl'impiegati negli altri Registri delle Corti, si Superiori che Inferiori, compresi i marescialli, i portieri ed i messaggieri—come pure gli Estensori delle Controversie, e che, a giudizio dei loro rispettivi Registratori, potrebbero, senza aggravio personale e senza danno del servizio pubblico, occuparsi nel disbrigo degli affari urgenti e straordinarj del Registro Civile.

2° Che si mettesse a disposizione del detto Registratore Civile una somma, io direi non eccedente cinquanta lire sterline per anno, per essere da lui spesa, nei casi di bisogni straordinarii ed urgenti, e pei quali non gli fosse riuscito di prevalersi dell'opera di impiegati negli altri Registri, e ciò a proporzione del bisogno e nell'ammontare, da essere dichiarato dallo stesso Registratore Civile e certificato da uno dei Giudici sedenti nella Corte Civile.

9. Ed in fine, per quel che concerne i Copisti al presente impiegati nel Registro Commerciale, nel caso della detta unione, è desiderabile che si esaminino i suggerimenti che da me saranno indicati in uno speciale *memorandum* relativo ai Copisti in generale.

(Valletta, 16 Decembre 1878.)

10. Fra le obbiezioni che si sogliono fare contro l'unione della Corte di Commercio alla Corte Civile, si annovera quella che risguarda i termini legali stabiliti per gli affari commerciali per un periodo di tempo più breve di quello che è fissato per gli affari civili, specialmente nei casi di appello. Questa obbiezione, a mio credere, è più apparente che solida, non solamente per le ragioni già accennate nella precedente osservazione sulla Corte di Commercio, ma anche perchè in nessun caso i litiganti possono soffrire realmente un pregiudizio in conseguenza delle abolizione della diversità tra i detti termini. Se il collitigante nella Corte di Commercio è rimasto *vincitore* colla sentenza, egli al certo non se ne appella, almeno per quel che concerne i capi *vinti*, ed egli, nel caso di *vincita*, può procedere per la esecuzione della sentenza ai termini degli articoli 278, 279 e 280 delle Leggi di Organizzazione e Procedura Civile, senza alcuna necessità di aspettare lo spirare del tempo stabilito per l'appello. Se il litigante nella Corte di Commercio è rimasto *soccombente* nella lite od in alcuni dei capi della lite, può senza dubbio rinunciare al termine legale per l'appello, ed interporre appello dalla sentenza o dai capi *perduti* anche immediatamente e senza aspettare il lasso dei fatali ad *appellandum*. E chè mai ragionevolmente potrà negare che i termini legali per l'appello non sono stati stabiliti a favore del *soccombente*, e che egli possa rinunciare, volendo, ad un dritto introdotto in suo favore ?

(Valletta, 26 Decembre 1878.)

V.

Second' Aula della Corte Civile di Sua Maestà.

1. L'esercizio della giurisdizione volontaria, come è al presente adempito dalla Second' Aula della Corte Civile di S. M., e come è organizzato coll'articolo 42 delle Leggi di Organizzazione e Procedura Civile, può essere attribuito, senza alcun inconveniente e danno pubblico, alla Corte di Appello di Sua Maestà. E nel caso di soppressione della detta Second' Aula, la giurisdizione volontaria dovrà essere esercitata dai membri della Corte di Appello per turno, compreso il Presidente.

2. Nel caso della detta soppressione, i doveri del Registratore della Second' Aula, anche come Archivista, potranno essere esercitati dal Registratore della Corte di Appello, e tutti gli altri impiegati nel Registro della Second' Aula Civile si potranno trasferire al Registro della Corte di Appello, senza pregiudizio dei dritti dell'attuale Registratore sin la sua promozione o sin che sarà messo sulla lista del ritiro ; e salvo ciò che si dirà sul Copista della detta Second' Aula nel *memorandum* sui Copisti in generale ; e salvo ciò che si riputerà proprio destinare, nel caso della detta unione, per contingenze, in ragione di legatura di libri, piccole spese, e *stationery*.

3. Io estenderei (nel caso della detta unione ed anche nel caso della unione alla Corte d'Appello delle Corti dei Magistrati in Seconda Istanza, secondo il *memorandum* Num. IV.), al Registro della Corte di Appello i suggerimenti espressi nel numero 8 del mio *memorandum* sulla Corte di Commercio.

(Valletta, 16 Decembre 1878.)

VI.

Le Spese Giudiziali.

Per l'oggetto di fare evitare giudizi vessatori e per fare assicurare il pagamento dei dritti di Registri delle Corti di Giustizia, io sono di opinione :

1. Che la disposizione del primo paragrafo dell'articolo 146 delle Leggi di Organizzazione e Procedura Civile, e secondo il quale non può essere ricevuto alcun libello che non sia accompagnato da una malleveria per le spese del giudizio, si debba estendere anche al caso di presentazione di citazioni (Articolo 173), quando l'oggetto in lite ecceda la somma di cinque lire sterline, o versi sopra beni stabili, o sia di un valore incerto ed indeterminato, come nei casi specificati nell'articolo 744 delle dette Leggi. La detta cautela è divenuta al presente necessaria, perchè non ostante il disposto dell'articolo 182 delle dette Leggi, stante la disposizione dell'articolo 185 adottata, per via di una ordinanza separata dopo il detto articolo 185 in origine esistente, nello attuale stato delle procedure e nella maggior parte dei casi, si procede per via di citazione e non di libello.

2. Che il Registratore, per cautelare i dritti del Registro, debba avere il dritto di rifiutare la malleveria indicata nel numero precedente, quando a suo giudizio, non sia idonea ad assicurare il pagamento dei detti dritti.

3. Che il detto rifiuto si possa fare dal Registratore o dallo ufficiale incaricato di ricevere il libello o la citazione, sia prima che dopo la presentazione del libello o della citazione, e che nel caso di insistenza della parte per la presentazione dell'atto, nonostante la dichiarazione della inidoneità del malleradore offerto, l'atto debba essere ricevuto coll'offerta malleradoria, e che il rifiuto del malleradore, come inidoneo, possa essere provato anche con un notamento sull'originale atto di essere stato il malleradore rifiutato come idoneo. Il notamento però dovrà essere datato e sottoscritto dal ricusante Registratore od altro ufficiale su menzionato.

4. Che nel caso del detto rifiuto per l'interesse del Registro la parte presentante l'atto dovrà avere tutti i diritti e dovrà avere tutte le obbligazioni contemplate negli articoli 919, 920 e 921 delle dette Leggi, e potrà essere applicata la disposizione dell'articolo 226 anche nel caso in cui la parte avversa non avesse rifiutato il malleradore.

5. Che nei casi di citazione in prima istanza per un oggetto non eccedente cinque lire sterline, il Registratore non debba ricevere la citazione senza un deposito di una somma a suo credere corrispondente alla spesa che potrebbe essere dovuta al Registro ed alla parte avversa, ed in nessun caso eccedente dieci scellini sterlini, per far fronte prima ai diritti del registro, ed in quanto al sopravvanzo per le spese della parte avversa, salvo il dritto per una somma maggiore nel caso che le spese eccederanno i detti scellini dieci.

6. Che nei casi di appelli da sentenze di una Corte Superiore in prima istanza essa Corte Superiore dovrà ricevere l'offerta malleveria, ma per l'interesse del Registro dovrà rifiutarla, quando la giudicasse non idonea, e nel caso del detto rifiuto si dovrà procedere come nel caso di rifiuto della malleveria, per parte di un appellante.

7. Che nei casi di appelli da sentenze di prima istanza pronunciate da una Corte Inferiore, l'appello dovrà essere dichiarato deserto, quando l'appellante almeno quattro giorni utili prima della trattazione della causa non avesse depositato una somma a giudizio del Registratore corrispondente alle spese dovute al Registro ed alla parte avversa, in un ammontare in nessun caso eccedente una lira sterlina, per far fronte prima ai dritti del Registro ed in quanto al sopravvanzo alle spese della parte avversa, salve le ragioni per una somma maggiore nel caso che la spesa sarà ad eccedere la detta lira sterlina.

Inoltre,

Per l'oggetto di far evitare giudizi frivoli e vessatori contro la Corona, e per l'oggetto di far diminuire notabilmente le spese che si sogliono annualmente votare per spese giudiziali, di certe procedure legali, di spese per ricupero di rendite, ecc., io suggerisco,

1. Che la disposizione dell'articolo 249 delle dette Leggi concernente la condanna nelle spese giudiziali sia estesa anche pel caso di cause contro la Corona od in favore della Corona.

2. Che conseguentemente sia soppresso l'articolo 489 delle dette Leggi, e secondo il quale non si possono tassare spese nè in favore nè contro la Corona. (Se mi ricordo bene, il detto articolo 489 fu adottato secondo la regola stabilita nel proclama del 10 Febbraio 1815, in quel tempo concordante colla legge inglese, e la quale al presente, se sono bene informato, è abolita.)

3. Che si faccia cessare la inutile pratica di fare pagare alla Corona i dritti per la presentazione degli atti giudiziali, nel mentre che gli stessi dritti pagati si riportano nuovamente nei conti a favor della Corona.

4. Che tutte le spese tassabili a favor della Corona secondo il numero 1 dovranno portarsi per intero a favor della cassa pubblica di queste isole, con essere portati ancora a favore della detta cassa le spese vinte in cause promosse da Dipartimenti non attinenti al Governo Civile di queste isole, ad eccezione di quelle spese le quali fossero state pagate dai detti Dipartimenti nel corso del giudizio, le quali, nel caso di vittoria del dipartimento e di condanna della parte avversa, dovranno ritornare al dipartimento da cui la spesa fosse stata erogata.

(Valletta, 16 Decembre 1878.)

Per l'oggetto di diminuire, in quanto è possibile, le spese che si sogliono fare, per accessi, testimonianze, vetture, interpretazioni, giurati, ecc. in occasione dei procedimenti criminali, sì nelle Corti Inferiori che Superiori, io suggerirei: che la Corte, sì Superiore che Inferiore, dovesse nel caso di condanna a pene applicabili ai reati (Articolo 7 delle Leggi Criminali) e nel caso di adozione delle misure contemplate negli articoli 340, 341, 345, 346 e 347 delle dette Leggi Criminali, condannare ancora l'imputato od accusato nelle spese del giudizio, anche in quanto a quelle che fossero state fatte in occasione della criminale istruzione (Articolo 351 e seguenti delle dette Leggi) quando la sentenza si pronunciasse dalla Corte Criminale di S. M. come pure suggerirei, che le dette spese dovessero essere esatte, a domanda del rispettivo Registratore della Corte contro il condannato o di suoi eredi col rimedio contemplato nello articolo 343, colla subasta degli immobili, e coll'arresto personale del condannato a proprie spese da incominciare dopo la espiazione della pena e da durare a beneplacito del Capo del Governo Civile ed a sua discrezione.

Nel caso che sarà adottato il detto suggerimento, sarà necessario emendare l'articolo 342 delle dette Leggi ed estenderlo anche al caso di procedimenti dietro rapporti e querele della Polizia, anche innanzi la Corte della Polizia Giudiziaria, come Corte di Criminale Istruzione, e con questo, che nel caso di un procedere della Polizia o di altri ufficiali del Governo che fosse stato vessatorio contro il privato, e nel caso in cui la Corte che avesse proceduto alla liberazione dell'imputato od accusato, avesse ancora dichiarato espressamente colla sentenza il procedimento vessatorio, dovrà coll'istessa sentenza condannare la Corona nelle spese giudiziarie a favor del liberato, salva l'azione civile per ulteriori danni ed interessi, e salvo in tutti i casi a favor della Corona il regresso contro l'Ufficiale, il quale avesse vessatoriamente proceduto ed il quale fosse stato dichiarato di avere proceduto con vessazione, e salvo ancora in tutti i casi il disposto nell'articolo 447 delle dette Leggi.

(Valletta, 16 Decembre 1878.)

Nel caso che sarà abrogato l'articolo 489 delle Leggi di Organizzazione e Procedura Civile, ed esteso a tutti gli affari criminali l'articolo 342 delle Leggi Criminali, e nel caso di decisioni a favor della Corona, come nella maggior parte negli affari civili sogliono essere, non solamente si avrà il vantaggio di fare ricuperare a favor della Corona una buona porzione delle spese che si fanno per conto della Corona, nei casi ordinari per procedure legali, ricupero di rendite, testimonianze, vetture, interpretazioni, accessi, giurati, ecc., ma ancora quelle spese che si fanno in casi straordinarj, come sono quelle che sono indicati nella prima partita della sezione sesta dell'Ordinanza di Appropriazione N° III del 1878 ed alcune di quelle delle quali si fa cenno nell'Ordinanza N° II del 1878 Sez° 5.

2. La condanna, nei casi criminali, a favore della Corona nelle spese fatte in occasione del giudizio, in una buona porzione dei casi, servirà ancora come un efficace rimedio per impedire e prevenire la commissione di reati e specialmente delle contravvenzioni. I delinquenti di cattiva condotta, presso di noi specialmente, temono più una condanna nelle spese che quella della riprensione od ammonizione e della prigionia ancora per breve periodo, come pure spessissimo della multa e dell'ammenda, e le quali danno loro il frequente vantaggio di vivere oziosi ed a spese pubbliche, e senza alcuna premura, in molti casi, di pagare l'ammenda o la multa.

3. Credo anche giusto di rimarcare, che per assicurare i dritti dei Registri ed evitare giudizj vessatori contro la parte avversa, il Registratore, nei casi contemplati nell'articolo 881 delle dette Leggi di Organizzazione e Procedura Civile, non debba accettare la petizione od il libello senza un deposito, almeno di dieci lire sterline, per fare fronte nel caso di soccombenza nella causa di ritrattazione, di dritti giudiziarj in primo luogo a favore del Registro, e per quel che riguarda il soppravvanzo a favore della parte avversa.

4. Mi pare ancora che non si dovrebbe in seconda istanza permettere di produrre prove che non fossero state prodotte in prima, quando si trattasse di sentenze liberatorie dalla osservanza del giudizio.

5. Mi pare che, in quanto alle dette sentenze, si dovrebbe emendare l'articolo 235 delle dette Leggi di Organizzazione e Procedura Civile, e che si dovrebbe rimettere in osservanza l'ultima parte, al presente abrogata, della Sezione III del Proclama N° VIII (in origine V) del 27 Giugno 1815.

6. Pel caso di riproposizione in prima istanza di una causa definita; sia in prima che in seconda istanza, con una sentenza liberatoria dall'osservanza del giudizio, io sono d'opinione, che il libello o la citazione relativi alla causa che si voglia riproporre non debba essere ricevuto senza il deposito di una somma corrispondente a quella che fosse stata spesa in occasione del giudizio precedente e già definito.

(Valletta, 16 Decembre 1878.)

Oltre che sono a peso della Corona tutte le spese che si fanno dalla Polizia Esecutiva, compresi i Sindaci nella loro qualità d'Ufficiali della Polizia, dalle Corti dei Magistrati della Polizia Giudiziaria e dalla Corte Criminale, per testimonj, vetture, ecc., in occasione di cause intentate per l'interesse pubblico, su azioni promosse per parte del Governo; ed oltre che non vi è alcun rimedio legale per ricuperare a favor della Corona le dette spese, nel caso di condanna contro gli imputati od accusati sono notabili, per quel che concerne i testimonj prodotti in loro proprio favore dagli imputati od accusati, gli articoli 332 delle Leggi Criminali e 382 delle stesse Leggi, e come il detto articolo 332 fu emendato, in quanto all'ultimo suo paragrafo, colla Ordinanza Numero IV del 1874, ed anche il penultimo paragrafo dell'articolo 364 delle dette Leggi.

Gl'imputati od accusati per i testimonii da essere citati in loro favore, ai termini dei detti articoli, non sono obbligati da alcuna legge in vigore ad alcuna spesa, nè per la domanda della spedizione della citazione, nè per la copia della citazione, nè per la esecuzione delle citazioni e nè anche per le vetture necessarie per tale esecuzione: e tutte queste spese, sì nel caso di una sentenza liberatoria che condannatoria, restano a carico della Corona, e senza alcun diritto di regresso contro gli accusati od imputati. Ed è osservabile, che nella maggior parte dei casi, gl'imputati ed accusati, per la ragione principalmente che non ne soffrono alcuna spesa, sono soliti di far citare de' testimonj, in un numero rimarchevole, e per lo più inutilmente e senza necessità o rilevanza della testimonianza, con dispendiare, mediante questo procedere la cassa pubblica, con occupare gli ufficiali dei Registri e della Polizia per le copie delle citazioni e per la loro esecuzione, e con fare perdere il tempo ai Magistrati, ai Sindaci, ai Giudici ed al Jury, e forse in quest'ultimo caso, per ragioni ovvie, in pregiudizio della amministrazione della giustizia.

Per rimediare a questi inconvenienti io prenderei la libertà di suggerire, pel caso in cui non si trattasse di persone povere, nel senso di essere dichiarato per mezzo di una legge speciale.

1° Che gl'imputati e gli accusati, quando volessero produrre nella causa dei testimonii in loro propria difesa, dovrebbero pagare alla Corona un dritto per la domanda che facessero per la produzione dei testimonj, e sia contemporaneamente alla domanda, sia che questa si facesse in iscritto, come nella Corte Criminale (articolo 381 delle dette Leggi) sia verbalmente. Il detto diritto a mio credere per testimonj nella Corte Criminale non dovrebbe eccedere uno scellino, e per le Corti Inferiori, due o tre pence.

2° Che le copie delle citazioni pei testimonj si dovrebbero preparare o fare a spese degli accusati od imputati, e presentare contemporaneamente alla domanda per la spedizione della citazione, con essere solamente sottoscritte dallo ufficiale destinato dalla legge per sottoscriverle.

3° Che nel caso in cui gli imputati od accusati volessero fare le copie delle citazioni per mezzo dell'Ufficiale o della Polizia o dei Registri delle Corti, dovrebbero pagare alla Corona il diritto stabilito per le copie e ciò prima della formazione della copia.

4° Che le spese necessarie per la esecuzione delle citazioni, comprese le vetture, dovrebbero essere pagate dall'accusato od imputato, prima della esecuzione.

Se si avrà, per mezzo del Soprintendente della Polizia dei Sindaci e de' Registratori, e specialmente del Registratore della Corte Criminale di S. M., un rapporto indicante l'ammontare delle spese fatta dalla Corona durante l'anno spirante, in occasione di citazioni di testimonj in difesa di accusati od imputati, si vedrà manifestamente che, su questo particolare è necessario dare qualche efficace provvedimento per sollevare la cassa pubblica e per reprimere e prevenire l'audacia degl'imputati od accusati.

(Valletta, 26 Decembre 1878.)

VII.
Copisti.

1. Pel caso di vacanza nello ufficio dei Copisti, per promozione od altrimenti, io suggerirei l'abolizione dello ufficio, come non necessario e di aggravio alla cassa pubblica, specialmente nel caso di pensione.

2. L'ufficio dei Copisti sarà inutile se le parti, contemporaneamente alla presentazione dell'originale, presenteranno al Registratore anche le copie dell'originale da essere notificate agli avversarj, sottoscritte dallo avvocato, con un certificato di essere conformi all'originale, e le dette copie dovranno essere senza spazj in bianco, senza abbreviature e senza correzioni, cancellature e postille, in buona carta e con buon inchiostro ed in caratteri leggibili. Il Registratore dovrà ricusare le copie quando non siano state fatte ai termini di questo regolamento.

3. Tutte le altre copie che si estraggono da originali già esistenti nel Registro e di atti giudiziarj che si spediscono dalla Corte stessa si dovranno fare dagli scrivani.

(Valletta, 16 Decembre 1878.)

VIII.
Estensori delle Controversie.

A mio credere, gli Estensori delle Controversie, in aggiunta ai loro doveri come sono contemplati negli articoli 61, 180, 605 e 712 delle Leggi di Organizzazione e Procedura Civile dovrebbero essere incaricati,

1. Dei doveri dei Giudici Supplenti ai quali si fa riferenza nella seconda parte dell'articolo 12 delle dette Leggi e per gli incarichi speciali indicati negli Articoli 616, 617 e 714 delle stesse Leggi.

2. Dei doveri accennati nello Articolo 48 delle dette Leggi, e per quel che concerne i testimoniali ivi menzionati.

3. Della difesa delle persone ammesse a litigare in "forma pauperis"—quando le dette persone non abbiano trovato un difensore di loro fiducia per difenderle.

4. Della condotta delle elezioni pel Consiglio di Governo come Commissionarii—giusta la legge elettorale, cioè l'Ordinanza N° I. del 1861, articolo 61 e seguenti.

Se sarà adottato il primo suggerimento io penso che i dritti tassabili ai Giudici Supplenti, giusta il numero 2 della Tariffa H annessa alle dette Leggi, dovranno essere percepiti dal Governo.

Se sarà adottato il secondo suggerimento, dovrà anche essere conseguito dal Governo il dritto fissato ai termini del numero 28 della Tariffa A annessa alle dette Leggi.

Se sarà adottato il terzo suggerimento, dovrà essere emendato il titolo nono del libro primo delle dette Leggi nella parte relativa agli avvocati ed ai procuratori pei poveri, come pure gli articoli 932 e 943 delle dette Leggi, e nel detto caso il diritto contemplato nell'articolo 940 delle dette Leggi dovrà essere conseguito dal Governo.

Pel caso in fine dell'adozione del quarto ed ultimo suggerimento, vi sarà, come è manifesto, un risparmio nelle spese delle elezioni, nella somma cioè che si dovrebbe pagare ai Commissionarii.

(Valletta, 16 Decembre 1878.)

IX.
L'Avvocato dei Poveri.

1. Come mi pare, nel caso di promozione dell'attuale Avvocato dei Poveri, il suo ufficio si potrà sopprimere.

2. I doveri di quell'ufficio, come sono indicati negli articoli 933, 934 e 935 delle Leggi di Organizzazione e Procedura Civile, potranno eseguirsi dagli Estensori delle Controversie, come si eseguono nel Gozo, secondo la Notificazione del 30 Decembre 1858.

3. I doveri del detto Avvocato, come sono contemplati nello Articolo 484 delle Leggi Criminali, potranno essere commessi dalla Corte Criminale, secondo la occorrenza, ad un avvocato idoneo e di sua fiducia, quando non fosse riuscito agli accusati di provvedersi di un avvocato, di loro scelta, e constasse, a soddisfazione della detta Corte, della povertà di tali accusati, mediante la prova del concorso di quei requisiti che una legge speciale sarebbe a determinare.

4. E per l'oggetto d'incoraggire gli Avvocati ad assumere il patrocinio di accusati, e per l'oggetto d'impedire che gli accusati si vessino con esorbitanti pretensioni di diritti pel patrocinio, e per l'oggetto ancora di far rimunerare dalla cassa pubblica gli avvocati scelti come sopra dalla Corte per gli accusati poveri e riconosciuti tali secondo la legge, io suggerirei, che dalla legge si stabilisca una moderata tariffa dei dritti pagabili agli Avvocati, nei casi criminali.

(Valletta, 26 Decembre 1878.)

ANT. MICALLEF.

APPENDIX D.

PROPOSED CHANGES IN THE ESTABLISHMENTS.

I.

Heads of Departments, &c.

Present Title and Salary.	£	Proposed Title and Salary (on retirement of the present occupants).	£
CHIEF Secretary to Government	1300	CHIEF Secretary to Government, not more than	1000
Auditor-General	500	Auditor-General and Director of Contracts	500
Collector of Customs	500	Collector of Customs	500
Collector of Land Revenue	500	Receiver-General	500
Cashier of the Treasury	350		
Superintendent of the Ports, with fees	300	Superintendent of the Ports	800
Controller of Charitable Institutions	400	Controller of Charitable Institutions	400
Superintendent of Police	500	Superintendent of Police	400
Registrar of Hypothecations and Notary to the Government	280	Chief Registrar	850
		Superintendent of Works	800
Commissary of the Monte di Pietà	240	Commissary of the Monte di Pietà	240
Public Librarian	200	Public Librarian	200
Superintendent of the Government Printing Office	190		
Deputy Collector of Land Revenue, Deputy Controller of Charitable Institutions, and Deputy Commissary of the Monte di Pietà, in Gozo	240	Deputy Receiver-General, &c. in Gozo	240
Assistant in the Chief Secretary's Office	350	Assistant in the Chief Secretary's Office	350
			£5280
		Estimated Saving	570
	£5850		£5850

II.

Judges, Magistrates, and Crown Lawyers.

Present.	£	Proposed.	£
President of the Court of Appeal	600	President of the Court of Appeal	600
Five Judges, at £500	2500	Five Judges, at £500	2500
Five Magistrates of Judicial Police in Malta, £200 to £310	1190	Three City Magistrates, £200 to £350 maximum	950
Three Magistrates of Judicial Police in Gozo, £180 to £200	560	Seven District Magistrates, at £177 in Malta and Gozo	1239
Seven Syndics at £177	1239		
Crown Advocate	550	Crown Advocate	550
Advocate for the Poor	100		
Assistant Crown Advocate and Advocate for the Poor in Gozo	65	Assistant Crown Advocate in Gozo	65
			£5854
		Estimated Saving	950
	£6804		£6804

III.

Clerical Establishments.

Present.	£	Proposed.
Chief Secretary's Office:—		
Chief Clerk	200	Chief Secretary's Office:—
Clerk No. 1	150	Three Clerks.
Clerk No. 2	140	
Clerk No. 3	120	
Audit Office:—		
Chief Clerk	180	Audit and Contract Office:—
Clerk No. 1	120	Three Clerks.
Clerk No. 2	100	
Treasury:—		
Chief Clerk	240	
Clerk No. 1	120	Receiver-General's Office:—
Clerk No. 2	100	Four Clerks.
Land Revenue and Public Works Department:—		
Chief Clerk	200	Public Works Office:—
Clerk No. 1	130	Two Clerks.
Clerk No. 2	110	
Clerk No. 3	90	
Clerk No. 4	75	
Customs:—		
Chief Clerk	180	
Clerk No. 1	120	
Clerk No. 2	100	Customs:—
Clerk No. 3	90	Six Clerks.
Clerk No. 4	80	
Clerk No. 5	75	
Clerk No. 6	70	
Port Department:—		
Assistant Superintendent of Ports	150	
Clerk No. 1	140	Port Department:—
Clerk No. 2	100	Five Clerks.
Clerk No. 3	90	
Clerk No. 4	75	
Police Office:—		
Chief Clerk	180	Police Office:—
Clerk No. 1	120	Two Clerks.
Clerk No. 2	100	
Clerk No. 3	75	
Charitable Institutions Office:—		
Chief Clerk	180	
Clerk No. 1	120	Charitable Institutions Office:—
Clerk No. 2	100	Five Clerks.
Clerk No. 3	90	
Clerk No. 4	75	
Monte di Pietà and Savings Bank:—		
Clerk No. 1	120	
Clerk No. 2	100	
Clerk No. 3	90	Monte di Pietà and Savings Bank:—
Clerk No. 4	80	Seven Clerks.
Clerk No. 5	75	
Clerk No. 6	70	
Clerk in Gozo	60	
Carried forward	£4980	

III.—*Clerical Establishments—continued.*

Present.	£	Proposed.
Brought forward	4980	

Public Registry:—	
Assistant Registrar	140
Clerk No. 1	110
Clerk No. 2	100
Clerk No. 3	90
Clerk No. 4	80
Clerk No. 5	75
Clerk No. 6	60

Court of Appeal:—	
Registrar	200
Assistant Registrar	110
Clerk	60
Copyist (paid by fees).	

Civil Court, First Hall:—	
Registrar	200
Assistant Registrar	120
Clerk No. 1	100
Clerk No. 2	90
Clerk No. 3	80
Clerk No. 4	75
Clerk No. 5	70
Clerk No. 6	60
Six Copyists (paid by fees).	

General Registry:—
   Three Assistant Registrars.
   Thirteen Clerks.

Civil Court, Second Hall:—	
Registrar and Archivist	170
Clerk No. 1 (partly paid by fees)	60
Clerk No. 2	80

Commercial Court:—	
Registrar	200
Assistant Registrar	120
Clerk No. 1	100
Clerk No. 2	80
Clerk No. 3	60
Three Copyists (paid by fees).	

Criminal Court:—	
Registrar	170

Civil Courts generally:—	
Computist	170
Clerk to Computist	80

Courts of Judicial Police:—	
Registrar, Civil Branch	160
Registrar, Criminal Branch	160
Registrar, Three Cities	120
Assistant Registrar	100
Clerk No. 1	90
Clerk No. 2	80
Clerk No. 3	70
Clerk No. 4	60

City Magistrates' Courts:—
   Two Registrars.
   Three Clerks.

Court of Gozo:—	
Registrar	120
Assistant Registrar	100
Clerk No. 1	90
Clerk No. 2	70
Clerk No. 3	60

Court of Gozo:—
   One Registrar.
   Four Clerks.

Total 85 Clerks, &c. and 10 Copyists paid by fees.   £9370

Total 63 Clerks, &c.* { Minimum £7260. Maximum £9690. }

*To be distributed as follows:—

	Minimum. £	Maximum. £
Fifteen First-Class Clerks, £190 to £250	2850	3750
Fifteen Second-Class Clerks, £130 to £180	1950	2700
Fifteen Third-Class Clerks, £90 to £120	1350	1800
Fifteen Fourth-Class Clerks, £60 to £80	900	1200
Three Probationary Clerks, £50 to £60	150	180
	£7200	£9630
Add allowances to two Registrars of the City Magistrates' Courts	60	60
	£7260	£9690

IV.
Professional Employés.

Except in a few cases, I have not attempted in the foregoing Report to make any precise recommendations as to reductions in the numbers, or changes in the salaries, of the numerous subordinate employés of the Government, such as policemen, prison warders, hospital servants, office messengers, and the like; and I have done little more than suggest the principles on which, in my opinion, its many and various professional employés should be dealt with. As regards the latter, however, the following lists may be useful in showing what are the classes of persons whose positions with reference to the Government require to be altered and better defined, with the help of such exact knowledge of details as the local authorities may be supposed to possess.

(1) *Legal Assistants.*
Reporter, Civil Court	£75
Reporter, Commercial Court	45 and fees
Reporter, Court of Appeal	45
Interpreter to the Civil Courts	60 and fees
Archivist of Notarial Acts	45 and perquisites

Whatever arrangement is made for the performance of these duties, those who execute them should be adequately paid for the work done, without having a claim to permanent employment or pension. The Keeper of the Archives, and so many of his staff as are retained, should be placed on the fixed establishment.

(2) *Medical Assistants.*
	£
Senior Physician in the Central Civil Hospital, and Visiting Physician at the Lunatic Asylum (also Professor in the University, £120)	145
Senior Surgeon and Accoucheur in the Central Civil Hospital (also Professor in the University, £80)	130
Resident Senior Surgeon in the Central Civil Hospital	75
Resident Junior Physician, ditto	75
Resident Junior Surgeon, ditto	70
Visiting Physician, Surgeon, and Superintendent in the Santo Spirito Hospital	80
Resident Assistant Physician, Surgeon, and Storekeeper, ditto	45
Resident Superintendent of the Ospizio	90
Medical Officer and Assistant Superintendent, ditto	70
Resident Medical Officer and Superintendent of the Hospital for Incurables	95
Resident Physician, Surgeon, and Superintendent of the Lunatic Asylum	100
Resident Assistant, ditto	70
Visiting Physician, Surgeon, and Superintendent of the Hospital and Ospizio in Gozo	50
Resident Assistant, ditto	55

As all these Medical Officers have the right of private practice, though some appear not to make use of it, it should be considered whether their numbers cannot be reduced, and all the services of those who are retained be utilised; and those whose stipends are only in the shape of retaining fees ought not to have claims to pensions.

Chief Police Physician, Inspector of Dispensaries, and Inspector of Addolorata Cemetery	240

I have recommended that this gentleman be retained as Chief Sanitary Officer, without his supplementary allowances of £60 and £30; and without the salary being continued to his successor.

Two Police Physicians, at £80	160
One Police Physician	56
Seven Police Physicians, at £50	350
Seven Police Physicians, at £40	280
Three Police Physicians, at £36	108
Eight Police Physicians, at £30	240

Of these twenty-eight Medical Officers only sixteen should be retained, at increased salaries, one at £100 and fifteen at £80 each, or £1300 in all. Except in the case of one, who receives £40 for assistance in the Sanitary Office, the allowances made to some of the Police Physicians (£150 in all) as Sanitary Officers, should be withdrawn. This arrangement will involve a total expenditure of £1340 a year, instead of £1344 as at present.

(3) *Public Works Office.*
	£
Chief Land Surveyor	240
Clerk of Works	200
Land Surveyor No. 1	170
Land Surveyor No. 2	100
Land Surveyor No. 3	90
Land Surveyor No. 4	70
Assistant Land Surveyor and Draughtsman	70
Draughtsman No. 1	90
Draughtsman No. 2	75

The appointment of a Superintendent of Works which I have recommended will supersede the post of Chief Land Surveyor. Such assistance as he requires from Surveyors or Periti should be rendered either by a reduced staff of permanent employés, debarred from private practice and adequately remunerated for their whole services, or by competent outsiders, paid by fees for such work as is actually done by them from time to time. The Clerk of Works and Draughtsmen, being exclusively employed in the public service, may very properly be regarded as members of the fixed establishment.

CPSIA information can be obtained
at www.ICGtesting.com
Printed in the USA
LVHW081347190422
716617LV00010B/483